HAVE SPIRIT, WILL DUCHESS

TANSY RAYNER ROBERTS

ISBN: 978-0-6454519-5-5 (ebook)

ISBN: 978-0-6457025-0-7 (paperback)

❀ Created with Vellum

For Elvira & Ruth
Whose novels I would read

And Madame Arcati
Who did her best under trying circumstances

CONTENTS

DRAMATIS PERSONAE

JUNO JUPITER, DUCHESS OF STORM, *a perfectly pragmatic pregnant heroine*

HENRY JUPITER, DUKE OF STORM *a heroic husband, not without his faults*

MR VANCE VON TRASK, *a husband with far more faults, conveniently deceased*

MRS MNEMOSYNE "MNEME" SEABOURNE, *a dear friend and confidante*

MR C. THORNBURY SEABOURNE, *a spellcracker of note*

ANTIOPE SEABOURNE, FORMER DUCHESS OF STORM, *a definitely deceased duchess*

MRS GALATEA "AUNT" SEABOURNE, *Juno's aunt-in-law, Mneme's mother, significant Seabourne matriarch*

CAPTAIN J. WILLOUGHBY BONES, *a privateer with a family connection, captain of the Caliban*

BOSUN BLYTHE, *a privateer with an entirely different family connection, boatswain on the Caliban*

MR DOMINIC VON TRASK, *former brother-in-law, sinister magister, possible necromancer and all around suspicious fellow*

MR BERTRAM VON TRASK, *silk merchant, father-in-law and all around terrible human being (so very, very deceased)*

QUEEN AUD, *monarch of the Teacup Isles, on the verge of a diplomatic alliance*

ALFRED, LORD MANTICORE, *the Queen's Minister, a terribly important gentleman, inconveniently in love*

PRINCESS LAENIA OF TREVENTAL, *a helpful young lady and terrible gossip*

PRINCE SAUVON OF TREVENTAL, *a fashionably floral fellow, and eligible royal suitor*

COMTE GEORGES OF ARUNIA, *a very keen royal suitor*

DUC RUDOLF OF GEDOS, *best of a bad bunch, we hope*

MR MARLBOROUGH, *a devoted valet with a particular taste in fashion*

BETTINA, *a most essential maid*

MR FARADAY, *a bookkeeper (deceased)*

DEAKIN, *the world's oldest footman (deceased)*

MRS EMMELINE HAWTHORN, *a housekeeper and qualified Medium (second class)*

ETOILE, *a Continental maid*

TALBOT, BELLINGS AND FREDERICKS, *a trio of butlers working for the Jupiter family*

MR CHALCEDONY THE ELDER, *a gentleman jeweller*

MR CHALCEDONY THE YOUNGER, *another gentleman jeweller*

RAFFERTY, *ship's cook on the Caliban*

HOBSBAWN, *a sailor on the Caliban*

LADY DORRIT, *a senior member of the Royal Society of Mediums (first class)*

MRS SMEE, *a senior member of the Royal Society of Mediums (first class)*

ALDERWOMAN GRENFELL, *a senior member of the Royal Society of Mediums (first class)*

MR ABERNATHY BROOKS & MRS RHEIA BROOKS, *Juno's parents*

AGATE, AMETHYST AND OPAL, *Juno's cousins, daughters of Aunt Ida*

THE CALM BEFORE

Fifteen months or so after becoming a duchess, Juno could confidently claim that she was nailing it.

Imperious manner in public, only softening in the presence of the most intimate friends? Check.

Extraordinary wardrobe, the envy of all? Check.

Gathering diplomatic connections and favours in order to progress her keenest causes and (on occasion) change the world for the better? Check.

Then of course, there was the private side of her new role: the care and maintenance of a deeply attractive, secretly dangerous and occasionally enigmatic duke.

She could not check that box, as being married to a duke was not a task one could ever feel was fully complete. A work in progress, you might say.

But oh, it was different this time around. *Wifecraft.* Juno had never imagined how much of a change it could make, to be fond of one's husband. To desire him in bed, to crave his kisses and his conversation, to genuinely care about his safety and whereabouts and happiness.

There was no other reason she would devote a perfectly lovely Tuesday afternoon to hovering in the bedchamber of Henry, Duke of Storm, observing (and occasionally interfering with) the packing of his travel trunk — a task usually left to a valet.

Mr Marlborough, Henry's valet, put up with a great deal in their household. Henry was no tyrant, liking to be liked far more than he cared about his orders being obeyed to the letter. Juno, on the other hand… well, her husband's valet had plenty of reason to bitterly complain in the kitchens about the Duchess of Storm.

According to Bettina, her most obliging intelligence-gatherer among the maids, he had already complained about her three times today. Juno hugged this knowledge to her, well aware of its value. She would never punish Mr Marlborough for snarky eye-rolling in the company of his fellow servants, but it helped greatly to manage her own feelings of inferiority that she could, at any time, let him know that she knew and thus shock that superior smirk right off his face.

Secrets gave one power. And power was a fashion that never went out of style. Juno intended to remain a best-dressed duchess in all senses of the word. It was a job for life, after all.

"Your peach cravat, my dear," she suggested lightly. "It goes marvellously with my apricot pelisse."

Henry, lounging on his own bed in a rumpled state while his valet and wife did all the work, offered her a teasing smile. "It does indeed, love. But your pelisse is not coming along on this particular journey. And neither, of course, are you."

"A gentleman's only hunting trip," she huffed. "One might think Lord Manticore had hand-calligraphed his own invitations proclaiming no wives allowed." She gave her husband a pointed look, which he pretended not to notice.

Because Mr Marlborough was a stellar valet, he did not at this point mutter anything unflattering about wives, but Juno could tell he was thinking it very clearly.

This was a little game they played. She pretended to accept whatever ridiculous excuse her husband came up with, and Henry did not put any particular effort into his lies, so that she did not feel insulted.

Such was the life of a wife whose husband served the Crown in matters of great secrecy, even after his supposed retirement from such tasks.

"Hardly fair of you, my love," said Henry affably, continuing the game. "Lord Manticore no longer has a wife to prevent from joining his revels." The Great Divorce had sent shockwaves through the aristocracy at the end of the summer, only a few months ago, with rumours surrounding the sudden end to the marriage of Lord Manticore, favourite to the Queen, and his wallflower wife Lady Persimmon.

"He is still a father," Juno said pointedly, her hand passing over the curve of her belly, so as to remind her husband of the future heir to the dukedom, a passenger *en route*. "As you are to be, soon enough."

Henry's face softened. Any reference to the passenger was a guaranteed win to any argument, and Juno wielded that particular tool without mercy. "Do not fret," he said, and gave her a great bussing kiss upon her lips without heed of the presence of the long-suffering Mr Marlborough. "I will not be gone long enough for you to worry."

As always, Henry's overwhelming sincerity was a little too much for Juno to take. She had spent years building up all her cynical armour, and here was a fluffy, kind-hearted husband who genuinely meant everything he said (except when lying badly about royal missions, of course).

It was a lot.

Juno sniffed now, and moved away from the circle of his arms, retaining her dignity. "Perhaps the violet breeches? The Queen always says you look so fine in those."

A tease, of course; she was not supposed to know that wherever Henry was off to this time almost certainly involved Queen Aud of the Teacup Isles, his patron and monarch.

"I have already packed the black breeches," broke in Mr Marlborough, looking alarmed.

"He's not going to a funeral," Juno snapped.

"Black is a classic look for gentlemen."

"Have you been reading those pamphlets by Basil Robucks again?"

"Of course I have," Mr Marlborough hissed, a sheen of sweat appearing on his brow. "Everyone has. He's a *genius of fashion*."

"A little unimaginative, don't you think?"

An outraged squeak emerged from the valet's pert mouth. He drew himself up in high dudgeon, and then flung himself into the master's dressing room. A moment later, the sound of him angrily ironing small-clothes filled the air.

"Darling," said Henry, swooping down upon her in one of his full-bodied hugs. "This trip isn't Mr Marlborough's fault. Try to keep your vengeful spirit to a dull roar."

"You love my vengeful spirit," Juno muttered into the side of his cravat. She hated how his hugs made her feel calm and kinder to the world. How dare they.

"Indeed I do." Henry drew back for a moment, and kissed her on the nose.

4

"I think I'll go to Storm North," she said, nestling herself against his chest. "Mneme is nearby, so I can interfere with her refurbishment of the manse. Perhaps it's time to consider some renovations of our own. That old nursery of yours is like something from another century."

"Are you sure?" Henry pressed. "There are so many more amusements here in Town."

"I don't want amusements without you on my arm," Juno huffed. "I want to *nest*."

Henry hesitated only a moment before kissing her again. "Whatever you want, my love. I'll be home again soon."

~

*B*efore portals were available to ladies — a recent and most delightful change of social convention — transporting the Duchess of Storm from their town house to their country seat might have taken weeks of packing, arrangements, hiring of swan-shaped boats, long rickety carriage rides and so on. A full production that could absorb most of a month.

Now, it was only the matter of commanding a small valise to be packed with her essentials, then stepping through the portal in her husband's study, along with Bettina — the one maid Juno could not do without. It barely took up the hour after luncheon.

Of course, it only took her half a cup of tea to remember how much she loathed being here at Storm North without Henry. In Town there were so many things to do outside the house — events to plan, promenades to make. A wife might occupy herself every day of the week without a husband on her arm. Here on the Isle of Storm, everything reminded her of Henry and his family legacy.

The dour face of ten generations of the Jupiter family glared out from every portrait on every wall. Locals adored the Duke of Storm and his family… but Juno still felt *new* here; the latest in a long line of duchesses. However welcoming the locals might appear, she was a minor accessory to the main event of the dukedom.

It did not help that she lived in the constant shadow of the other Duchess of Storm, Juno's immediate predecessor. Antiope Seabourne (Henry's late mother) was a figure so majestic and magical that her presence inhabited every room in the house, despite the Duchess being three years in her grave.

After a little initial resistance, Juno had finally begun to put her own mark on the house, encouraged by her husband. She refurbished rooms and changed around colour schemes, furniture, and so on. Still, the footprint of her mother-in-law weighed heavy in the dust.

Juno lived in Antiope's house, carried her title, slept in her bedchamber and even wore her wedding ring upon her finger: a mighty square-cut ruby set into a thick band of gold, handed to every duchess by their duke over the last several generations. Here at Storm North, the ring felt heavier than usual.

She should be grateful. She *must* be grateful. Henry had no idea what he was saving her from when he first put that ring on her finger. He probably did not even know it was enchanted. Somehow he managed to perform daily magic without the deeper fascination with the subject that everyone associated with his mother's side of the family.

At least the passenger was not so troublesome as they had been during the early stage of Juno's pregnancy; for the first three months, she had barely been able to eat more than flatbreads and ginger tea. She felt better now, more robust, though her face in the mirror remained gaunt in comparison to her swelling belly, and it was hard to get back into the habit of eating foods that had caused such havoc on her system only recently.

The ancestral ring of the Jupiter family was too loose on Juno's finger. Every time her friends came to visit, they brought cakes in a manner that they probably thought was subtle.

Soon after her husband departed for Lord Manticore's 'hunting trip,' it began to rain heavily. Juno stood at the window of the day parlour, missing Henry fiercely and embracing all the dramatic potential of a thorough sulk.

Tomorrow, she would be bright and build baskets for the poor. She would call on her friends, and write cheerful letters. But today, for a single rainy afternoon, she would indulge her melancholy.

Outside the window, lightning flashed. The trees around the house silhouetted themselves against Juno's vision.

"Tea, your grace?" murmured Bettina behind her, essential as ever. Juno might not have much of an appetite, but there was always room for tea.

Juno turned away from the window. As she did so, the ancestral ring of the Jupiter family fell from her too-thin finger and hit the parquet floor with a 'crack.'

"Oh no!" gasped Bettina. "Is it broken?"

Juno stooped — still able to do this for herself, at least, she was not so far advanced in pregnancy that such a manoeuvre was impossible — and scooped up the ring in her hand. "No harm done," she said aloud, only to realise she was wrong. The ruby was loose in the setting. As Juno prodded at it, the jewel jumped free. "Damn it."

Was the ring warm in her hand, or had the rest of the room grown suddenly cold around them?

Bettina sucked in a breath.

"Don't fret," Juno said quickly. "It's the setting, that's all. The ruby is sound. Any goldsmith can mend it."

Any goldsmith who was also a magister; it was the enchantment Juno was worried about, not the ring.

"Send someone for Mr Thornbury," Juno added. "Mr Seabourne, I mean. He'll be at Tempest Manse, or else the Hare and Wicket. Send a footman to each. Hurry, child."

With a squeak, Bettina spun and fled, leaving the Duchess of Storm alone with her broken ring, and a deep sense of foreboding.

Rain continued to drill down outside the window.

~

A few minutes later, the door of the parlour opened. Relieved at the haste with which Thornbury had come to her aid, Juno looked up, only for her breath to catch wildly in her throat.

Antiope Seabourne, Duchess of Storm, swept into the day parlour: a solid woman with a high arrangement of bejewelled red hair, wearing a red and white striped gown Juno had once spotted hanging in the attic.

At least, her spirit swept into the day parlour. If you knew enough to recognise the signs, you might notice that her feet hovered a half-inch off the parquet floor, her voice had a certain hollow echo to it, and *oh yes*, her skin was pale enough that you could almost see the pattern of the wall-paper through her face. Juno knew the signs better than most.

"Who are you?" commanded the spirit of Antiope Seabourne, her voice vibrating the room.

Juno clutched the gold ring and the loose ruby tightly in the palm of her hand. She curtseyed with the same level

of deference she had been taught to use only for the
Queen.

"I am your daughter-in-law, Duchess," she said. Peers
used the title in that way with each other, something Juno
had struggled to absorb when she first acquired her own
title. In public, Juno was supposed to call Henry, "Duke."

If a Duchess of Storm was not the peer of another
Duchess of Storm, then the term 'peer' surely meant
nothing at all.

"Nonsense!" declared the other woman, proceeding
into the room with the same momentum as a galleon at full
sail. "Why would my son be so foolish as to choose a bride
without my approval?"

Juno cleared her throat. "I'm rather afraid, Duchess,
that he did so because you were dead."

2

TO WEATHER THE STORM

*J*uno saw her first ghost at the age of twelve. A weeping maid in the garden of her mother's house, always at the same hour of the day. Only when she went up to the poor creature did she notice that the uniform was old-fashioned even by her mother's standards… and then, when she put a hand on the crying girl's shoulder, it passed right through.

Ghosts were rarely good conversationalists. Mostly they got stuck on a single moment or issue to do with their fleshly existence. Some called out the name of their killer, over and over. Others worried about a task left undone. There was a pale, sickly old woman in the house of Juno's Aunt Ida who muttered constantly about buttons while staring into a cupboard full of table linens.

But then there was the child in the apothecary's garden, who had fallen to his death and still had a line of blood along his temple. He not only talked in full sentences, but noted what was going on around him: remembering details about the lives of the breathing up to a week after overhearing them. He was a great source of gossip to Juno, and she often found an excuse to call by and learn more about the apothecary's three mistresses, his wife's screaming arguments with herb suppliers, and all manner of town talk.

Most ghosts remained locked to a place they had died, or else a place that meant the most to them when they left life. Sometimes they haunted an object, not a place. Juno inherited her grandmother's hairbrush, which brought with it the unexpected and entirely unwanted shade of her actual grandmother.

She hid the hairbrush in an attic of a friend's house and never regretted it.

Still, ghosts were not especially plentiful in the town of Grey Mare on the Isle of Thyme, where her family resided. Her father was the son of a gentleman who had mildly disgraced the family by becoming a solicitor instead of a priest; her mother was the daughter of a draper who was deeply dedicated to appearances. A great-aunt's inheritance was the only reason Juno was able to afford a 'coming out' at the age of 19, alongside her wealthier, prettier young cousins.

She was presented to the Old Queen without incident, though her first visit to Wistworia Palace was alarming. So many people gathered in one place; so many of them dead.

So many of them with something to say: it turned out that ghosts surrounded by the constant activity of the breathing were more likely to remain aware of themselves.

Juno was in her element during her first Season. She made friends and collected invitations to all manner of great houses. She was introduced to luxuries fancier than any her own family could dream of. She learned from her new friends, affecting not only a refinement in her accent, but in her manner.

If some of those friends were not among the breathing, well, that was no one's business but her own.

She did not catch a Lord, as her mother had hoped, but she did capture the eye of Bertram Von Trask, a wealthy widowed silk importer with three grown sons who was looking for a daughter-in-law to run his house. Letters were written; offers were made.

The first time that Juno and her parents took tea with the Von Trasks, she saw the faded shade of Bertram's wife standing behind her three sons, silently screaming.

It was a sign Juno should have heeded; but by that stage, there was little she could do to halt the process of her first betrothal.

~

*W*illiam, the quiet one, was considered too young to marry; he was a year older than Juno herself.

Dominic, the elder one, spent every spare minute immersed in his magic studies, and showed no interest in marriage. (A near miss, Juno thought to herself, for there was something in Dominic's glassy gaze she did not trust at all.)

Vance, though, the middle son, who did the books for the family business and was all charm and affability… "This one will give me grandsons," his father said, all smiles and back-slaps.

Vance was his least favourite son, but Juno did not know that yet.

~

*O*nly a few weeks after her wedding to Vance, still dazed from the warm promise of her honeymoon and feeling that her life had finally begun, Juno learned the truth of the Von Trask family business.

Armed with a housekeeping list of what stores were to be found in the cellar, she went down the steps with a lantern, and found herself faced with an army of ghosts.

"Bertram Von Trask ordered me killed," said a brutish looking man.

"Dominic Von Trask broke my fingers," said a merchant with a knife-slash on his throat.

"William Von Trask knocked me out with one punch," said another, lying on the ground. "What am I doing here? My wife is expecting me home."

A woman in a kerchief and apron sat upon the ground, arms wrapped around her knees. "Vance Von Trask said I cheated the family of six silver pennies," she whispered. "How did he know? Why did he say anything?"

Juno turned around and left the cellar, clutching the list to her chest.

She could not leave.

She was a part of this family now.

She had a cellar full of reasons to know that running away was not an option. In any case, where could she run?

~

*T*hree years. Three years of managing the Von Trask town house on the Isle of Glass, staying out of the family business, and doing her best not to notice if a breathing person was taken down to the cellar.

Vance was charming and attentive, as husbands went. She told herself that he did the books. His hands must be clean. (It was easy to tell herself such things, if she stayed out of the cellar.)

Still, Juno learned more about their business than she ever intended, thanks to her household management. She arranged dinners when asked. She overheard conversations on her way out of rooms.

Bertram grew careless around her, used to her presence. Taking his daughter-in-law's compliance for granted. He let more slip than he should, and Juno hated him for it; it made her feel like she was furniture.

She learned that Dominic was the fixer. Bertram was involved in every stage of his own business: the shipping of precious silks from various countries, the trading to local suppliers, bribes and excises; and the hidden underbelly beneath that business, the secrets that must never be uncovered by the Queen's agents. When he found a problem he could not immediately handle, he sent in his ruthless eldest son.

William was the enforcer. He was young, but solid and ridiculously tall; his father had caught him sneaking off to an illicit boxing ring as a boy, and put his muscle to use.

Vance was the one they all ignored and despised. He did the paperwork, and complained to his wife about how little his father and brothers respected him. He, too, let details slip from time to time, forgetting that his wife had never agreed to be part of a family business grounded in manipulation, violence and the art of cheating the system.

Two years into Juno's marriage, young William vanished. No one saw him go; no one knew where he went. There was a note, but Juno was never allowed to know its contents. All she knew was that he had finally escaped his father, and the ghost of his mother screamed less, once he was gone.

Dominic looked more haunted than ever. Vance was

included far more in business conversations with his father. Juno had never been more certain that her situation was hopeless.

❧

The best times in Juno's marriage were when the Von Trask men packed up and went to their hunting lodge on the far side of the Isle of Glass. With them gone, she could breathe again. Attend tea parties with her friends who lived nearby, buy gifts to send to friends and cousins for the naming ceremonies of their babies (secure in the knowledge of her own hidden contraceptive charm, her most vital rebellion). She could move about the house without worrying she might come upon further evidence of her father-in-law's criminal activities.

Apart from the ghosts, obviously. But at least they were confined to the cellar.

A month after her third wedding anniversary, Juno returned from a tea party to find Bertram and Dominic unexpectedly returned from the lodge a few days early, their faces grim, tumblers of brandy in their hands.

She stood there for a moment in her bright green damask gown, feeling foolish and wondering where her husband was.

"Call the dressmaker," said Bertram flatly, when he took notice of her at all. "You're a widow now. You must dress the part."

Dominic looked as though he was going to say something, but he stared into his brandy instead.

❧

*A*fter the funeral, Juno went to her rooms and began to pack. She rather liked the rustle of stiff black taffeta; there was an armour about it, being a widow. People in the street startled to look at her, as if she was a little terrifying.

One could fill a gown like that with all manner of convenient pockets, tied on and removed as necessary, to provide storage as well as ballast. Another secret rebellion was that every time she added a new black taffeta pocket to her gown, she lined it in the merriest, most cheerful printed cotton she could find. No one need ever know how free she felt, now that Vance was dead.

"What are you doing?" said a voice at the door. Dominic. His ability to enter a room soundlessly never failed to chill her.

"You know what I'm doing," Juno said calmly, laying her garments into the trunk. "I'm going home to my father's house."

"This is your house."

Faraday had warned her; the ghost of Bertram's previous accountant, the man who had trained Vance in bookkeeping. He hid in the attic still, as if the sturdy walls of a broken wardrobe would save him from being found and physically thrown out of a window, as had occurred five years or so before Juno's wedding.

"I know Bertram's plans," Juno sighed. "Do you even *want* a wife? I didn't think you liked women."

He'll be keeping you in the family, Faraday whispered to her when she was scouring the attic for sewing notions. *Leave while you still can.*

"I don't like anyone," Dominic said flatly.

Juno huffed and flung herself around, letting her exhaustion and misery show on her face. "I'm done, Dom.

16

Don't do this. Don't keep following every order without thinking for yourself. What do you want from life? It's not me. And I know it's not standing in the shadow of your father. What is it *you* want?"

His blank face startled, as if no one had ever asked him that question.

Juno returned to her packing. "Tell him what you like. Tell him you put a spell on me to hold my tongue, or wipe my memory. Just bloody do it. Cast your spells. Do your worst. Whatever it takes to get me out of this house. And then consider what you want out of life. Whether being a part of the family business is worth what he makes you do."

She had gone too far, she knew, too close to hinting she knew the secrets of the cellar.

To her enormous relief. Dominic turned and left her alone.

The Von Trask family did not stop her, as she let herself out the front door and headed to the ferry dock.

She never quite lost the feeling that at any given moment, they might come for her.

~

Juno returned home to Grey Mare on the Isle of Thyme, to familiar comforts and small rooms in her parents' shabby but comfortable town house.

She burned everything she had acquired during her marriage except the wedding ring (kept in a small iron box) and the black taffeta gown with its many, many pockets. None of the possessions she moved back into her family home had any connection to her dead husband or his family. She would not be haunted by any Von Trask.

A few months later, at the earliest point it was deemed socially appropriate to switch out her black taffeta widow's gown for something in grey and violet, she burned that too. Pockets and all.

After she had raked the bonfire to ensure that no scrap remained, Juno found her father standing on the threshold of the back door, facing the small garden of their town house. "My dear," he said faintly, staring at her. "Don't tell your mother. I wouldn't want to upset her."

"Don't tell her what?" Juno asked, but her father dissolved before her eyes, and she heard a cry of anguish from above.

Ghosts, always ghosts. She could never be entirely free from them. Every event in her life was marked by death.

At least her father had not felt the need to stick around; some ghosts had an easier journey onwards than others.

~

*a*few years later, Juno heard that Bertram had died, and that Dominic was back at college, immersed in postgraduate magister studies. The Von Trask Silk Shipping empire vanished as if it had never existed.

She received a letter from a bank, informing her that her dowry had been returned, along with some rather startling numbers. She now had the means to fund a pleasant retirement for her mother, and set up her own household, should she wish.

Her cousins had other ideas.

"Do the Season again," said Agate, bouncing a round child bundled in antique lace upon her knee. "You loved the Season."

"The frocks, the parties," agreed Amethyst, whose own children were running around the lawn, playing pirate.

"Catch yourself a rich husband — or a handsome poor one, if you prefer."

Juno had confessed a little of her marital trials to her cousins. "After last time," she said now, "the last thing I want is to submit myself to a husband, let alone another powerful family."

"So take a Season or two to enjoy yourself and *don't* capture a husband," scoffed Opal, the cousin who had died in childbirth three years earlier. "You're a widow of independent means and you are alive. You can choose your own fate."

She drifted away, as she usually did, chasing the children while Agate and Amethyst stared at Juno expectantly.

"I suppose there's no harm in purchasing a frock or two," she conceded reluctantly.

They whooped and cheered at her.

~

Two Seasons later, Juno found herself caught up in the most ridiculous scheme: to capture the heart of Henry, Duke of Storm. There were parties and frocks, magical croquet. Garden parties. House parties. An abduction, and a rescue.

And finally, most unexpectedly, there was a proposal.

~

"Marriage is a messy business," said Henry Jupiter, wiping cake crumbs from his sleeve.

Juno tsked at him. "It's not marriage that created this particular chaos," she said, glancing around at the wreckage strewn across the lawn of Shellwich Standing, the Seabourne family estate. "It's a world that tells women their only value is in who they marry. Eligible dukes are practically designed to fuel that fire. I'm surprised there wasn't murder done."

There had been so many women in that temple, throwing cakes and creating havoc; some of them were even alive.

"Are you *not* interested in a husband?" asked Henry, with a warm smile he probably thought was charming. "I could have sworn you were courting me."

Juno swatted him with a napkin, adding to his cake crumb situation. "Sometimes the game is amusing, regardless of the prize."

He gasped, pretending to be shocked. "Madam, are you suggesting I'm no prize?"

She narrowed her eyes at him. "Sir, you know exactly what you are."

～

From the moment Henry Jupiter, Duke of Storm, put his ancestral ring on the finger of his bride, Juno saw no ghosts.

She saw no ghosts in the weeks that followed.

It had now been one year and three months, and the first ghost she saw in all that time was when the ancestral ring broke, and her mother-in-law stormed into the day parlour.

Juno had half-hoped it was her happiness with Henry that had ceased the hauntings; but no, it had been the enchanted ruby on her finger all along. And now...

Now, the honeymoon was over.

3

IN THE EYE OF THE HURRICANE

The Teacup Isles were awash with duchesses, which was to say there were several at any given time, plus a dowager or two. If one were to gather them all in the same room along with the countesses and marchionesses and even the Ladies (as opposed to ladies), one would find few who had anything positive to say about a nobody like Juno snagging the coveted hand in marriage of the Duke of Storm.

It was better that way. Juno was able to create her own presence as a duchess, without constantly being told by her peers that she was getting it wrong. (She had her own mother for that, even if their communication had dwindled to letters every three months.)

Still, she occasionally wondered what it would be like, to have a dowager at her shoulder. If Henry's mother was still alive, was it possible she would have helped to sail the new Duchess of Storm through the murky waters of her early public appearances? To offer quiet but encouraging words of advice, when they were discreetly in private? Or would she have made everything ten times worse?

Now, of course, Juno knew the truth. Having a duchess as a mother-in-law was hell on earth.

~

"Who changed the wallpaper in the violet day parlour?"
"What happened to the peacocks on the lawn?"
"Who are you to sit in the Duchess's salon?"
"This is my wardrobe. Send me my maid, instantly."
"Where is my son, where is my son, where is my son?"

~

The ghost of the late Antiope, Duchess of Storm, was clearly distressed. It often took spirits like that, when they first awoke and found themselves in the presence of the living. She had not yet internalised that she was dead, and that the world had moved on.

It made Juno wonder about her ring. She had guessed that the ancestral ring of the Jupiter family prevented her from seeing ghosts; there was no other explanation for her circumstance that made sense.

Now she wondered if the enchantment actually prevented the presence of ghosts altogether. Antiope was not acting with the confidence of a ghost long-established in her own home. She was a first-day banshee, all howl and confusion.

Juno was sympathetic, but it still gave her a headache.

She sent most of the servants away for an unscheduled day off, hoping to minimise situations where they might catch her talking to thin air, or filling a room with pained silence and constant flinching from the Duchess of Storm's many diatribes.

Nowhere was safe. Ghosts tended to be restricted to the

22

place where they died, the place they felt most at home, or some significant object from their life; they could not haunt people, thank goodness, or she might still have her last set of in-laws trailing after her.

Unfortunately for Juno, the late Duchess of Storm (was she officially a dowager after death, or did she retain the title as she had held it at the end of her life?) felt at home *everywhere* in Storm North. She followed Juno to the kitchens and the attics and the bottom of the garden, demanding answers to her questions every step of the way.

"Why have you not sent for my son? Why have you not written to my *sisters*? They both have the ability to see ghosts, you know."

That stopped Juno. It was the first acknowledgement from the (damn it, she was just going to say dowager and assume no etiquette expert was going to come out of the woodwork to tell her how wrong she was) Dowager Duchess that she knew she was dead.

"I can write to your sister Galatea," Juno offered. What she did not say was: *your other sister is locked up for crimes against my husband, and I feel you would not enjoy being enlightened as to that fact.*

Antiope, the Dead Dowager Duchess, was a testament to the fashions of an earlier era: her hair, high and glossy, was clearly a wig when you got close: an expensive wig in natural red instead of the more common white that was in fashion two decades ago, covered in pins and brooches. Her face was powdered, and her bosom presented on a pearl-encrusted shelf thanks to hardworking corsetry.

She leaned in Juno's direction, her green eyes narrowing. Ghosts rarely retained something as substantial as eye colour; the Dowager Duchess must have an incredibly strong spirit. "Do it," she commanded.

Juno felt her own spirit revive. "Say please," she ordered in return, matching stare for stare.

The Dowager's confidence faltered and for a moment, she was entirely transparent. "Please write to my sister and tell her I am here," she said in a voice that in no way sounded like a plea.

"I was going to the library anyway," Juno said calmly, and led the way.

~

TO: *MRS GALATEA SEABOURNE, SHELLWICH STANDING, THE ISLE OF MEMORY*

Dear Aunt Seabourne.

["*You call her Aunt Seabourne, what kind of peasant stock are you from?*"]

Your late sister Antiope, the Dowager Duchess of Storm...

["*DOWAGER? Don't tell me Henry finally found a wife. Not you, obviously. You have more of the torrid mistress look about you. He always did like actresses.*"]

...is currently awake and haunting my home.

["*Who do you think you are to write about indelicate matters with shameless abandon?*"]

24

Please attend on her at your earliest convenience.

Cordially yours,

Juno, Duchess of Storm.

["*What.*"]

~

With some satisfaction, Juno melted her own seal and stamped it hard, while the ghost screamed in denial over her head.

Once she sent the letter on its way, it was time to immerse herself in some useful research.

That meant finding the right books. She barely remembered what she had done with the personal belongings she had brought to the marriage; she had definitely shipped a crate full of her old research books on ghosts and hauntings to Storm North, along with a few personal keepsakes. It amused Henry, at the time, to learn that his new wife had such a quirky interest.

By then, his ring was already on her finger, and she had not seen a ghost in weeks; Juno had no particularly interest in the books other than not wanting to leave them where her mother might come across them. If they had not been shelved here in the Great Library, then where?

Storm Bolt, of course. There were three libraries in their town house, and Juno had barely set foot in any of them. That must be where Henry had stored her old books.

~

"*W*hat on earth are you doing, interloper? Is there no scandal to which you will not stoop?"

Finally, Juno had found somewhere the Dowager would not follow her: through the portal at the back of the library. Henry had suggested they install his and hers portals in the dressing rooms, as he'd had one in his boudoir long before they were allowed for ladies. Juno preferred the privacy that came with keeping the access points to their home downstairs.

"I'm popping over to Storm Bolt to fetch a book," she said lightly. "Would you like to join me, Duchess?"

"That is a gentleman's convenience," gasped the ghost. "How dare you bring your hoydenish ways into my house?"

"My house," corrected Juno with a brief smile, and stepped through the portal.

Oh, the blessed relief. It was like moving through a warm bath that massaged you all the way through — and, most importantly, it silenced the voice of her mother-in-law.

~

*J*uno found the books she needed in the Duke's Library, the smallest of the three, which opened from Henry's billiards room. This was where former Dukes of Storm had shelved their most manly tomes over the centuries: those concerning fishing and hunting, along with a discreet lower shelf of vintage pornography, charmed to look like a dull and out-dated encyclopaedia of facts about the Civil Service.

Henry himself appeared to have added a shelf full of

rather charming romance novels and several illustrated books of mythology, as well as her own collection of texts about hauntings and ghosts. It was the only shelf that had been dusted recently.

Juno had rather hoped never to need these again, but she was touched to see her books given pride of place. She had dragged them along to her last marital home as well, but kept them in their crate so that none of the Von Trasks would ask awkward questions about why she took such an interest in the spirit world.

She needed to get the Jupiter ring fixed, and quickly. Still no sign of Mr Thornbury Seabourne, her husband's pet spellcracker — the footmen Bettina sent in search of him had reported that he and his wife Mneme were away from home.

It was a blow, as she had been hoping at least one of them could come to her aid. After all, it was Mneme's aunt haunting her halls. Who else could she trust with the mending of the ring?

There was only so much help she could gain from books. What Juno really needed was a person to give her a cup of tea and tell her that all would be well. Possibly, though she would never admit it aloud, even a hug would do the trick right now.

She had been craving hugs rather more since the passenger came aboard, which was a terrible side effect of which no one had warned her.

"Can I be of assistance, your Grace?"

Juno glanced up to see Deakin, one of the elderly retainers that Henry liked to keep about the place, because Storm servants refused to retire or some such nonsense. Light duties and local colour.

"Deakin," she said. "Can you have this shelf of books boxed up and sent to…" Juno paused, and blinked.

"Deakin, didn't you die peacefully in your sleep several months ago?"

"Yes, your grace," said the world's oldest footman.

"That will be all, Deakin, thank you."

Frustrated, she shoved the books she was holding back on to the shelf. She could come back for them any time. Nothing was to be gained from dragging them from pillar to post, and besides she had nowhere to go. Liesl was in Town, but living in far more bohemian quarters than Juno would have been able to survive even before she became a duchess. Who else could she turn to? Her cousins? *Mother*?

Surely things were not that dire.

The last book did not quite fit on the shelf. Juno tugged impatiently at it, only to see a buff envelope flutter out of its pages, and fall to the floor.

It had been tucked into *A Girl's Guide to Wayward Spirits*, no wonder she hadn't found it before. She hadn't cracked that particular cover since she was fourteen; it had little to offer but games for tea parties, and some basic spiritualism charms. Barely worth hanging on to all these years.

The letter, though…

Slowly, Juno made her way to the floor — her centre of gravity was not what it was, but the passenger did not completely have her in its thrall yet — and picked up the envelope, turning it over. When she recognised the handwriting, spiky and black, on the other side, she let go as if it were a hot kettle.

The letter was addressed to Mrs Juno Von Trask, in her husband's hand. Her *first* husband. The wrong husband.

"Damn it," Juno swore, backing out of the room.

All this time. She had been so careful to ensure she took nothing from Vance's home that had belonged to him, nothing that could be even slightly haunted by him or his father. Nothing but the books and clothes she had taken with her to that first marriage, plus one dress of black taffeta which she had later *burned*, pockets and all.

Behind her, Juno heard the crack of billiard cue against ball. *The billiard balls were packed up on a shelf, because Henry was away and they got so very dusty when left out.* Slowly, she turned, dreading what she might see.

The ghost of Vance Von Trask, Juno's first husband, leaned over the billiard table. Nicely dressed, of course, his slender form wrapped in a suit slightly too expensive for him. He always liked to look smart. Neatly trimmed dark beard — no reason for him to ever shave again. That same, smarmy smile. So very pleased with himself. Confident, as long as his father was nowhere near.

He struck again, cue against ball, though they were as ghostly and translucent as the hands that grasped the cue. "Wife," he said in an indolent voice, as if they had only been apart a few hours, not years. "We have *so* much catching up to do."

4

AN ILL WIND THAT BLOWS
NOBODY ANY GOOD

When Juno finally caught her breath, it tasted of fury. Truly, she had never realised quite how angry she was about her first marriage until this very moment. "I have nothing to say to you, Vance."

The ghost of her late husband leaned back, surveying her like he used to when she tried on a new dress. "Don't you want to know the last thing I ever wrote to you?"

"No," she snapped. *Yes*. "It's been six years. You have been dead for six years, Vance. You are irrelevant."

Never tell a ghost they are dead. It was a firm guideline found in several of those books on the shelf. Juno did not care. This was an unacceptable haunting and it had to stop right now.

She had taken so many precautions. She had thrown her old wedding ring into the sea, because an iron box was not safe enough. She had burned her mourning dress…

"And look how far you've come." His mouth twisted up, and there was the Vance she remembered. The scowl behind the smirk. Petulance beneath the charm. "Duchess of Storm. Your mother must be so proud."

"How do you know my title?"

He smiled with all his teeth. "You think I was raised yesterday? I've been haunting this room for years. Ever since the books were unpacked on to that shelf. Lots of magic resonance in an old house like this. I can even hear what's said in the room next door."

Ugh, Henry's billiards room — which he insisted on calling the cigar parlour, thanks to family tradition. He entertained his gentlemen friends there. And, apparently, talked about his wife when she and the ghost-preventing wedding ring were not around.

Was it only Storm North that was so tied to the enchanted ring that ghosts never haunted there, even when she and the ring were elsewhere?

"For some reason," Vance went on. "Never when you're in attendance. Almost as if you've been trying to avoid me."

Juno rubbed her thumb across the empty fitting of her ring, thinking of the ruby currently secreted in a small box within one of the many pockets she still liked to tie on to favourite gowns, though now they were stitched by a fine dressmaker instead of herself. "You realise," she said aloud, "the easiest way for me to resolve this embarrassing situation is to throw that letter of yours on the fire."

"No!" Vance looked genuinely terrified. "Don't," he said wildly. "When I'm not here — I go *there*. I hate it there. Don't take this away from me."

Juno hesitated. "There?" Was she about to learn some secret of the afterlife?

Now it was Vance who looked haunted. "The house," he admitted. "My father's house."

Oh, *there*. "I wouldn't want to visit either," she said. "But surely it's been sold by now. Since your father passed away…"

31

"Ha!" Vance looked strangely triumphant. "Yes, indeed. He's not haunting the place, if you were wondering. Apparently, he died with a clear conscience and no unresolved concerns. Typical."

Juno's eyes narrowed. "Have you been reading my books?" It was rare to come across a ghost who was so knowledgeable about how haunting actually worked.

Vance did not answer her question, which was probably for the best. It would only raise further questions, and then they would end up in a conversation, which was the last thing she wanted.

"Dom sold the property to some nice, normal family," he said instead. "There are grandchildren, and pets. Every year it moves further and further away from anything that reminds me of my life. My family."

"I'm sure there's still a grim remnant or two of the Von Trask family history, clinging to the walls," Juno said sharply. "Have you tried the cellar?"

Vance's eyes met hers, held fast. "I knew you knew. All those years. And you never said a word."

"I didn't trust you. I still don't. I don't want to deal with this, Vance. Whatever it is you need, I can't give it to you. I owe you nothing." It took everything Juno had not to lay her hands over her stomach, as she usually did when she felt anxious or distressed. The passenger was none of Vance's business. Thank goodness the fashions of the day allowed for loose fabric beneath the bust. Not that her current bust was not itself a walking advertisement as to her state of being.

"I'm not myself there," Vance said, returning to his soliloquy about his family home. "I'm washed out, colourless. Barely a ghost. If you destroy that letter, I'll lose what I have left of myself."

"You're not making the argument you think you are," she said flatly.

"Juno, the letter is important. I don't know why — there's a lot about my life I don't remember." He pouted, leaning against the cue. "I thought you liked me better than this, for a start."

"You thought that in life, too."

"I don't remember what I wrote to you. But it feels important. Perhaps it's the reason I'm here." He smouldered at her, working his handsomeness and charm for all it was worth. It was irritating. Juno could not imagine what her younger self had ever seen in him. "I need you to find out who murdered me, and why," he added. No please, of course.

Juno laughed shortly. "Are you serious? Vance, it was your father or your brother. There's no mystery to it. Yours was the least mysterious death I can possibly imagine."

He looked a little hurt at that, as if his terrible family was news to him. "I don't know *why*."

"*I* don't care," she insisted. She had lived so long now, without him looking at her. This was the last thing she needed today.

"Wife," Vance said pointedly. "Will you at least read the letter? Perhaps if I know exactly what I wrote, it will be enough to, you know." He made a vague hand gesture, all flourish. "Send me on my way to the other side."

Juno sighed. She had wasted so much time when she was younger, doing small tasks for ghosts who crossed her path, hoping to bring them the peace they craved. Sometimes it worked. More often, it led to frustration and misery and yet another street she could never walk down again, or public building she could never enter.

This would all be over soon. She would get her ring fixed. And if that meant Vance was banished to a puppies-

and-rainbows version of his family home whenever she was in residence at her husband's townhouse, that was none of her concern.

"I will read the letter," she conceded. "And then our business is done, Vance."

"We'll see," he said, waiting.

Juno stooped and picked up the envelope. She remembered these: crisp and business-like. They were scattered all over the Von Trask house. Letters were sent, payments were made, threats were codified. All within the same buff-coloured rectangles of paper. Her father-in-law ordered them by the hundred.

There was a wax seal on the back, barely a dribble; she broke it. Six years, and she would be the first to know the last thing her husband wrote to her.

First husband. Late husband. Former husband. For a moment she filled her thoughts with Henry, red-haired and strong and joyous. His laugh. His kind eyes. His sheepish expression when he thought he had let her down. Oh, yes. She had traded up.

She took a breath, and tore open the letter.

❧

***Juno, if you are reading this, I am dead.
Get out of this house, to a place of safety. Contact
JWB of the Miranda, if you need help.
Do not trust my brother.***

❧

*T*t was oddly touching, that he had been so concerned for her. She held the paper up so that Vance could read it.

"I don't want it to have been Dom," he said, sounding sombre.

Such a sad indictment of their family: it made more sense to him to have been murdered by his father than his brother. It certainly made more sense to Juno, though of course it was always Dominic's job to fix his father's messes. Perhaps it had been both of them, working in concert.

"If your father gave an order, Dominic would have obeyed it," she sighed.

"That's not comforting."

"Is that my role here, to comfort you? I have a life, Vance. A new life. So far away from what we had together. Much better, as a matter of fact." Why yes, she was prepared to be cruel, if that meant escaping this tiny room crammed with books and ex-husband.

"JWB," Vance muttered. "The *Miranda*. That sounds like a ship's name. We had shipping interests, of course, but… I wish I could remember. We could find it, couldn't we? The ship."

"We?"

"If you carry the envelope, you can take me anywhere with you…"

"No!" she said loudly, startling them both. "I won't do it. I won't hare around the Teacup Isles questioning ship captains to solve your murder, Vance. No one cares if you were murdered or not. I'm done here."

She put the letter back into its envelope; took *A Girl's Guide to Wayward Spirits* back off the shelf in order to lodge the letter back inside it.

"You really won't help me," Vance said, sounding wounded. "After everything…"

"I owe you nothing," said Juno, and walked away. Head held high.

She was the bloody gods-damned Duchess of Storm, and she would not be haunted by the past like this. She would not be haunted at all. She would mend her ring, and close this whole sorry chapter.

If that meant pretending to herself that her first husband had had the grace and dignity to stay dead, then so be it.

5

A TEAPOT IN A TEMPEST

Unwilling to spend any more of the day dealing with her dead husband or her dead mother-in-law, Juno practically flung herself through the Storm Bolt portal. She was transported directly to the front hall of Tempest Manse, where she was relieved beyond all compare to find Mr and Mrs Thornbury Seabourne recently returned from their latest expedition to purchase wallpaper or haunt auction houses for new furniture, or whatever else they did with their time these days.

Thank goodness they were back. It was terribly bad manners to portal in to someone's home without their express permission, but Juno was running out of houses where she felt safe.

"My dear," said Mneme, startled at her arrival. She was still in her outdoor pelisse and bonnet. "We just got your note and were about to come over to Storm North. What on earth is going on?"

For possibly the first time in her life, Juno wanted to both cry upon *and* hug a person at the same time. It was most unlike her. "Tea, I think," she managed to request. "And cake, if at all possible."

~

"Ghosts," Mneme repeated, clutching her teacup to her chest. Her eyes sparkled with curiosity. "Really?"

"You're a Seabourne," said Juno. "Surely you've heard of ghosts."

"In stories. Never — *really*, my aunt is haunting your house right now?"

"Feel free to visit," Juno said with a wave of her hand. "She seems to think your mother would be able to see her. Perhaps you also have the family knack."

Mneme blinked, several times. "I'm sure I would have — *my mother*, you say?"

The drawing room at Tempest Manse was beautifully decorated, with ivy-patterned wallpaper and comfortable furnishings. Which was fortunate, because the rest of the house remained something of a building site.

When Juno married Henry last year, she acquired the friendship of his closest cousin, Mnemosyne. After Mneme's own recent marriage to Mr Thornbury, Henry's personal spellcracker and occasional partner-in-service-to-the-Crown, the Duke and Duchess of Storm had arranged for the couple to live close by, on the other side of the village.

Tempest Manse had been the home of magisters who served the Isle of Storm and its Duke for generations, even before the Teacup Isles was a queendom, when each island was independently governed by its own Duke or Countess or Earl or Lady.

The manse had been somewhat neglected for a generation or two, probably because the Jupiter family were perfectly capable of supplying their own magic instead of hiring magisters to do it for them. Henry's enthusiasm at restoring the house for his two favourite people had rather got away from him, and the project had blown out from its overly-optimistic timeline.

Still, Mneme and Thornbury seemed content living in the chaos of floors-to-be-polished, gaslamps-to-be-installed and doors-to-be-rehung. Still honeymooning in their hearts, bless them.

It was a great comfort to Juno that no one was currently haunting Tempest Manse; perhaps the ongoing renovations were too disruptive for the spirit world to handle.

If she could solve her current mother-in-law problem and former-husband problem with a rumpus of new flooring and wallpaper, she was prepared to make that sacrifice.

"You've *always* seen ghosts," repeated Mneme, having difficulty wrapping her head around this surprise. "You never said a word about it."

"One doesn't," Juno said impatiently. "Being able to see the dead is not a popular form of magic among the aristocracy. Do you know how many high society dinner invitations are extended to necromancers? *Very few*. If I cared for telling fortunes at village fetes or befriending spinsters with esoteric hobbies, I might be more inclined to mention it." She did not like the look of startled pity that flitted across Mneme's face, and so she did what she did best: making light of any situation. "Besides, it was no longer relevant by the time you and I were friends. I haven't seen a single ghost since my wedding day. Until now."

Thornbury, a quiet presence beside his wife, examined

the Jupiter ring with great interest, turning it and the loose ruby over in his hands. "This is a fascinating piece. I knew it had protective properties, but Henry never mentioned anything about warding off ghosts. You believe it kept actual hauntings at bay, not only your perception of them?"

"At Storm North, perhaps," said Juno, thinking of Vance. He was quite comfortable in the role of ghost, compared to her newly risen mother-in-law. How long had he been hovering in that extraneous library, waiting for her to call by? "Can you fix it for me?"

Thornbury looked apologetic. "I'm so sorry, your grace. My skill is in spellcracking, not the repair of enchanted objects. Besides, this is a legacy talisman, belonging to the Jupiter estate." He tipped the ring over, showing her a tiny stamp on the back of the setting. "The maker's mark of Gundrow's. It is under warranty for as long as the mark remains. No one else is authorised to repair the spell."

"They have a boutique in Town, at least," said Juno, relieved. "I won't have to set off to some ancient questing mountain or anything like that."

"You shouldn't be questing anywhere," said Mneme sternly. "You're supposed to be retiring at home. You need rest and good meals, not adventures."

"Funnily enough, with an elderly duchess haunting one house, and my first husband haunting the other, home is not feeling all that restful right now." Juno leaned her cheek against a cushion. "Perhaps I could stay with you while my ring is being repaired."

She caught a startled look between husband and wife.

"Of course, you're always welcome," said Mneme, biting her lip.

Juno sat up straighter. "You're going somewhere?" Oh,

she was nine kinds of idiot. Of course they were going somewhere. Lord Manticore's false 'hunting trip.' If Henry was off on a royal mission important enough to disregard his retirement, it was only natural that Thornbury should join him. It was only a surprise that he was not already at her husband's side. But surely… a *gentleman's retreat*, Henry had said. No wives allowed. "You too, Mneme?"

From the look on her friend's face, Juno had failed to conceal her wounded feelings. Drat this passenger, who always brought her emotions more readily to the fore. She only hoped that when the wretched creature was in the nursery where it belonged, she would no longer feel so constantly on the verge of tears.

"The Queen requested my presence," Mneme murmured. At her husband's disapproving *tsk*, she rounded on him. "I'm not going to lie to Juno, Thornbury. She has not suddenly become an enemy of the Crown just because Henry is playing the protective papa."

It was the passenger, then, who had ruled Juno out of this particular adventure, not any particular failing as wife or duchess. It was a relief to have that confirmed, though she would certainly raise the issue with her husband upon his safe return.

"I should get the ring to Gundrow's before they close," she said now. "The sooner the better."

"Finish your tea. I'll check whether they have a direct portal," said Mneme, getting to her feet and heading out to speak to her housekeeper. "We want to avoid you walking in the rain."

"I'm not made of spun sugar," Juno called after her. "People don't melt, even in my condition."

"She's worried about you," said Thornbury, amused. "Henry was hoping she'd be able to keep you company while we were away. We only just learned that…"

"Yes, yes. The Queen wants Mneme at her side. Don't we all?" Juno leaned forward. "Do you know how I might locate the crew of a ship from several years ago?"

Thornbury raised his eyebrows. "That's an odd request."

"Is it."

"Wouldn't have anything to do with a certain haunted letter, by any chance?"

She frowned at him. "I don't have to explain myself to you." The words *I'm a duchess* hung in the air between them, though fortunately she had the presence of mind not to speak them aloud.

"And I don't have to answer your question."

Drat it. Thornbury was always so amiable when Henry had a request of him. She had forgotten he was also one of the few people capable of saying 'no' to the Duke of Storm.

"I'm not going to go haring off on some wild adventure like the rest of you," Juno wheedled. "I simply need to corroborate some facts."

Thornbury eyed her suspiciously. "If you feel you must investigate your first husband's death…"

"I most certainly do not!"

"Can you at least wait until Henry and I return?"

"I have better things to do than running around doing chores for Vance Von Trask," Juno scoffed. "But surely I can look up the name of a ship without falling into dire peril."

"I'm flattered you think me a repository of nautical facts…"

"Who else was I to ask, my housekeeper? Mrs Hawthorn still looks down on me because I refuse to accept starched sheets. It's like tucking myself up in a paper envelope at night. And none of the butlers give me

42

so much as the time of day when the Duke is not around to glare them into submission."

Thornbury relented, but only slightly. "If the ship in question is registered with the Queen's service, you'll be able to look it up in the Shipping Almanac in your own library. If it is not, then *please* wait until Henry has returned to make any further investigation."

Juno gave him the brightest, sweetest smile. "I plan to make absolutely no investigation," she informed him. "Honestly! I thought the whole point of portal magic was that no one had to care about boats any more!"

"Ah," said Thornbury, looking uncomfortable again. "Well, there are still some locations inaccessible by portal."

"Such as the location of your secret mission with my husband?"

"You may think that, Duchess. But I couldn't possibly comment."

6

REDECORATING UP A STORM

The rain had ebbed by the time Juno crossed the village on foot to return to the majestic country manor of Storm North, refusing Mr Thornbury Seabourne's offer to escort her. The house looked no less ominous with clear skies above it.

She was starting to feel very tired, as she swept back in the front door, but not so tired she did not notice the wrong flowers growing in urns outside, the wrong carpet in the entrance hall.

Every change she had made to the house since her marriage, wiped away in a few hours.

"Oh, your grace!"

One of the Continental maids appeared, close to tears, wearing a uniform that Juno had retired on her second day as a duchess. "Things just keep changing. Mrs Hawthorn says the house is haunted."

"It is indeed," said Juno. Mercredi? Ophelie? Etoile. "Etoile, I told you all to take the day off and vacate the house."

Etoile sniffed. "Yes, your grace, but Mrs Hawthorn said

a few of us should stay, you should never leave a house without servants, not even when it's shut up."

Mrs Hawthorn. The elderly housekeeper was almost as much of a thorn in Juno's side as her dead mother-in-law.

"I will speak to Mrs Hawthorn," Juno said grimly. "But yes, as it happens. The house *is* temporarily haunted. Do you have somewhere you can go for a day or two? Otherwise I can send you through to Storm Bolt."

"I have a friend in the village," said Etoile, biting her lip.

"Then go, quickly. Do not return for two days. Is anyone else about?"

Etoile shook her head. "Bettina wanted to wait for you to return, but Mrs Hawthorn sent her through to Storm Bolt already. The rest of the servants will be back by dinner."

"I'll have to put up some kind of sign to warn them off." Juno shooed the maid away. So, Mrs Hawthorn thought she could deal with a haunting, did she? No one's secret recipe for autumn pudding was that powerful.

Antiope, the late Duchess of Storm, descended the great staircase, majestic in the family sapphires (how did a ghost retrieve them from Juno's jewel case, or were they merely the memory of sapphires?) and a floor-length, wall-wide gown in matching blue and silver. Her wig — out of fashion, even for the older ladies of court — was silver to match, with blue butterfly ribbons all around. "So," she said in a voice that chilled Juno to the bone. "My son married a widow. Were there no virginal young ladies for him to choose from?"

Juno breathed in. The air crackled around her. Her comfortable teagown (let out by her modiste to make ample room for the passenger) shivered against her skin, and was suddenly replaced by a stiff, ruffled gown in mourning black. Taffeta. *Widow's weeds.* In an instant, she was taken back to the memory of that awful time when she first returned to her mother's home, unable to tell her everything that had occurred with her husband.

Damn it, she had burned this dress.

This would not do. This was entirely unacceptable. "This is my house now," Juno said in a ringing voice. "Your time is over, Antiope."

"Ha," said the former Duchess of Storm. "Is that what you think, stealer of sons?" The ghost raised her arms, and the sweeping curtains over the long windows shifted from red velvet to soft blue linens, as fresh as the day they had first been mounted (as opposed to the worn, faded fabrics Juno had replaced).

Ghosts shouldn't be be able to do this. They should not be able to control the living world so effortlessly. Juno had met poltergeists before, creatures who could tip a glass off a shelf, or nudge a feather from room to room. But this?

She remembered something, some footnote from her youthful research about how those who had wielded power in life, the strongest of magisters, might be especially formidable in the spirit world… especially if haunting a location where their identity was especially strong…

Antiope Seabourne was a perfect storm.

"This is not your house," Juno said again, and stalked away to the kitchens, bunches of black taffeta rustling stiffly against her legs.

The merry laughter of her mother-in-law followed her all the way down.

～

here were no cooks or maids in the kitchens, but Juno found her housekeeper conspiring in the butler's pantry with not only Talbot, butler of Storm North, but also Bellings, long-time butler of Storm Bolt, and the rather youthful Fredericks, who supervised the six staff at Storm Rest, a tiny hunting lodge in the midland mountains.

"Mrs Hawthorn," Juno said crisply. "Gentlemen. Might I join your council?"

"Oh, your grace, such a to-do!" huffed Mrs Hawthorn. "I do believe there's a ghost in the house."

"There is indeed," said Juno. "I'm handling it."

"With respect, your grace," said Talbot in his usual grave, measured tone. "The usual protocol is to send word to the Royal Society of Mediums, and to the nearest temple."

"I see," replied Juno. "This has happened before?" It was somewhat a relief to learn that there was a protocol for this. Juno should have known that butlers planned for every eventuality.

"Not in *this* house," Mrs Hawthorn said staunchly. "The very idea!"

Juno gave them all her own steely duchess gaze. "I believe this situation will be resolved once the family ring is restored. I have an appointment in Town, after which I will know precisely how long we must endure the attentions of our visitor. Please close the house *completely* this time, Mrs Hawthorn. Anyone who remains on site may be in danger."

She had to hope that the Dowager Duchess would not actually hurt a member of the current Jupiter household, but anything was possible.

~

"Where are you going now, little widow?" demanded the Dowager Duchess as Juno marched with determination towards the main library.

"I have a book to borrow," Juno replied between gritted teeth. She would not linger in this house longer than she had to, even if it meant remaining in the horrid black gown that her mother-in-law had imposed upon her. She had wardrobes aplenty in the townhouse, at least.

The haunting had not affected the library yet — clearly the Dowager Duchess had little attachment to this particular room. Which was odd, because Juno was rather fond of it. She had spent many hours here even before she made Storm North her home; it was a popular morning retreat for all the ladies who had attended a certain house party.

When all this was over, she should invite her friends to stay with her. Liesl would surely come, if she could be dragged from her current insalubrious abode with her new companion Perdita. Perhaps Mneme and Letty Agnew and some of the other ladies from that house party might join her. Her cousins: she had not seen Agate or Amethyst in ages. Juno felt the need to surround herself with women who were neither dead nor dedicated to sneering at her.

At least the Duke had devised this particular library with all the modern charms, to make life easier. "*Shipping Almanac,*" Juno said aloud, and waited as the books shivered and tapped against each other.

A narrow leather-bound volume came whizzing up out of the deepest stacks, hovering in the air before her.

Voice-activated library spells were one of her favourite indulgences. Henry was a little too fond of them, of course, and had managed to bruise himself several times by calling for too many books at once, in too hearty a manner.

Oh, she missed him. What she would not do to have him at her side, offering comforting embraces, humorous asides, and standing up for her against his mother... assuming he would, of course, take Juno's part in the conflict. She had no idea what Henry's relationship with his mother had been like, except what little she could glean from the ghosts's forceful personality.

"*Miranda*," she said next.

The pages of the book flicked back and forth wildly, settling in one page in particular.

> **_Miranda_, royal privateer vessel**
> **Decommissioned after storm damage.**
> **Captain: Decius Hartigan.**
> **First Mate: J. Willoughby Bones.**

"JWB," Juno murmured to herself. So, the note from Vance meant something real, even if he did not remember why he had felt the need to write it down so many years ago.

Not that she cared. She was not here to solve his puzzle. She had a dead mother-in-law to evict from her home.

Still, when Juno left Storm North for her town house via portal, she took the *Shipping Almanac* with her. Just in case.

Luckily, the haunted widow's gown was still equipped with the pockets she had added to the garment in her previous life; there were at least six attached, and one of them was large enough to swallow the *Shipping Almanac* whole.

~

The Arcade of Ladylike Dainties was one of the premier shopping destinations of the Isle of Town, home to all manner of modern and antique delights. The enclosed street was beautifully decorated and tiled, so that the prettiest boutiques might sell their wares to ladies without the lanes between shops filling up with old oyster shells and other detritus.

It was Juno's favourite place to promenade during the Season, especially if there was scandal in the air.

The crown of the arcade, at the very centre of the most decorated archways, was Gundrow's: the oldest jewellery emporium in the Teacup Isles and quite the most exclusive.

Juno would never have dared to darken their doors when she was Miss Brooks or Mrs Von Trask, even with her terrifying father-in-law paying the bills. But the Duchess of Storm, of course, was an established patron of Gundrow's. No one would imagine her to purchase jewels anywhere else.

(Juno had been there exactly three times, smiling and projecting confidence while secretly expecting to be hurled out on her ear at any moment.)

Today, she was ushered in by a staff of polite young greeters. Furnished with tea and cakes, she found herself seated in the prettiest corner of the receiving hall downstairs, surrounded by perfectly-lit glass cases full of treasures.

Mr Chalcedony the Elder presented himself to her: an elderly gentleman jeweller who looked nearly a ghost himself, in a starched cravat so perfectly stiff and white it might have been carved from marble.

He examined the ruby and the empty setting of her

ring through a pocket peering-glass, tutting to himself for some time.

"It can be fixed?" Juno asked at last, no longer able to bear the silence.

"The ring, of course. It is a matter of nothing to re-set the jewel. But the curse…"

"Curse," she repeated. "Surely… charm?"

"It was a curse originally," said the jeweller. "That's what is so fascinating about the Jupiter family. Follow the House of Storm back a few generations and they were all quite wild, murderous creatures. The very worst magisters of the century before last were mostly in the employ of your husband's ancestors. Death by curse was the most common cause of death in that family for generations."

Juno squirmed uncomfortably. It had never occurred to her that, of her husband's bloodlines, it was the Seabourne family that might have been the civilising force. "So, the ring was cursed?"

"Indeed. It's a fascinating field of study, curses that were intended to be malignant, but emerged with positive outcomes. My great-nephew did his dissertation on that particular subject. In fact, let's get him in here."

It was getting late. The Arcade of Ladylike Dainties must be closing soon. But Mr Chalcedony was fired up now, summoning more tea, more cakes, and his great-nephew Mr Chalcedony the Younger, who appeared with a fresh face of enthusiasm.

Juno sighed, and settled more deeply into the most comfortable couch in the world, as the two jewellers debated back and forth the history of various curses placed upon her wedding ring over the last five hundred years.

Several of them sounded highly alarming, though she was assured they were no longer present, having long drifted away from an active presence in the ruby.

"Fascinating," muttered Mr Chalcedony the Elder, after consulting several records. "The banishing of ghosts is a comparatively recent addition to the ring, and it wasn't I who added it."

"Nor I," said Mr Chalcedony the Younger.

"Well, it wouldn't be you, young pup. No, there's no record at all of that particular curse being officially laid upon the ring by anyone at our establishment, and it was not present at the ring's centennial service, forty three years ago, though I believe we did note the curse's presence when his grace brought it to us before your wedding last year. As very old and celebrated customers, we chose to forgive the breaking of the warranty agreement."

"Can you repair the curse?" Juno asked. "Whether or not it was added officially, it's now part of the heritage of the ring. Isn't it?"

"True, true," muttered Mr Chalcedony the Elder. "That's heritage magic for you. Why, the number of highly illicit curses we've been asked to endorse over the years, just because they've been around for longer than you or I…"

"Seven days," said Mr Chalcedony the Younger, with an air of finality.

Juno blinked. Had she dozed off? "Seven days," she repeated. "To repair it completely?"

"It's a complex curse made up of several threads of enchantment that need to be properly woven. We won't be able to begin until after the full moon. And of course, some of the ingredients are difficult to come by."

This, at least, Juno knew how to handle. "You will find the Duke of Storm's account is more than generous."

Mr Chalcedony the Elder coughed discreetly. "Not a matter of funds, your grace. One ingredient in particular is something that we find highly challenging to source. Delays might be inevitable…"

"And what ingredient is that?" Surely the whole point of marrying a wealthy duke was that anything could be bought. Juno could not stand the thought of her homes being haunted any longer than necessary.

"Transient vapour," explained Mr Chalcedony the Younger, sounding a little too excited. "It is the essential ingredient that turned the original curse of isolation and death into a talisman banishing ghosts from the wearer's vicinity… and given its connection to your country seat, banishing ghosts completely from the grounds of Storm North."

"Transient vapour," Juno repeated. "How does one find it?"

The young jeweller held up a small, empty glass bottle. "One captures it at the moment that a ghost is banished from our plane of existence."

"Banished. By force?"

"Not at all!" He seemed almost offended at the thought. "It is an act of kindness, not of violence. The spirit must be assisted to move, as it were, *to the other side* by concluding their business in the earthly realm. The vapour left behind by such a process can be captured in glass."

Juno sighed. "And it is essential to the curse?"

"Vital. We can source it ourselves, of course, but it will take time. Hence, seven days at least before the curse can be restored to the ring. Possibly longer."

"You don't have ghost-handlers on staff who could be encouraged to work faster?"

"This is a very rare curse, your grace. I only know the theory, I'm afraid, not being blessed with the sight myself. But if you could find someone with the ability to see and communicate with ghosts, then I believe the most efficient practice is to solve whatever problem or question keeps a spirit tethered to the mortal world."

Both jewellers looked at Juno expectantly. She regretted having confided her own abilities to them.

"My mother-in-law's problem is me being married to her son," said Juno pointedly. "I don't feel that resolving any of that is in my best interest."

"Well," said the jeweller, a touch awkwardly. "Perhaps some other ghost with a more easily solved problem could be consulted?"

Juno sighed, very deeply. *Of course.*

~

*B*ack to Storm Bolt, and the gentleman's library behind the billiards room. "I blame you for this, entirely," said Juno, smacking the *Shipping Almanac* down on a nearby shelf.

Vance appeared in the tapestry chair set into the reading nook, looking smug. If only one could slap a ghost. "Wife," he said, looking her up and down, taking in the ruched black taffeta, and heavy sleeves. "Nice dress. Very appropriate for your station as a widow in mourning."

"Shut up," she snapped. "I will investigate your letter, and I will find out which of your terrible relatives murdered you. In return, you will do me the colossal favour of vacating my house *and* this mortal coil, forever."

Vance's face shifted a little. For a moment, he looked almost vulnerable. "Take me with you," he requested quietly.

Juno laughed hollowly. "What use do you think you can be?"

"I'm the only witness to my own death. Surely if you find out any further clues, it may trigger my memory."

She glared at him, then snatched up the letter that so vividly displayed his handwriting. "*Fine*. I will keep this in my pocket. On the condition that you do not appear in my presence or speak to me unless I first summon you. I will not endure your presence a minute longer than is absolutely necessary."

Vance Von Trask lowered his head in a polite bow. "I am at your grace's mercy," he said.

"I mean it, Vance. One snotty line, one surprise appearance in my bedchamber, and I will throw your letter overboard, and start over with a different ghost."

He held her eyes for a moment, surprisingly sincere. "I'm grateful, honey bee. I will do whatever it takes to earn your trust."

She scoffed. "Start now. With silence."

7

ANY PORT IN A STORM

*J*uno slept little that night, in the enormous bed she usually shared with Henry. When she rose, and went to her dressing room, she found herself staring at the stiff black gown provided to her by the former Duchess of Storm.

She was not a widow. Not any longer. And yet, if she was to spend the day combing the docks and ports of the city in the search of a ship full of privateers, it might be best not to dress in her usual manner.

(If nothing else, she did not want anyone speculating on why the current Duchess of Storm's wedding band was missing.)

Why not play the widow? She knew from experience that there was a power in mourning dress. People saw the colour and the cloth, but did not meet one's eyes.

And so, wearing rustling black taffeta gown paired with the plainest bonnet she owned, Juno left the house by the back entrance, with a letter from her dead first husband stored securely in one of the gown's many pockets.

*A*ccording to the *Shipping Almanac*, Captain J. Willoughby Bones now commanded a ship named the *Caliban*.

The Isle of Town had several dockland areas, but the most common port for ships with affiliation to the Queen was Crownport, on the outskirts of the south end of the city. Juno emerged from a public portal in the Seadog Inn, and began her investigations. As luck would have it, the *Caliban* was berthed, though scheduled to leave later today.

The boards of the jetty were damp and slippery. Juno took extra care as she walked; there were times when she was almost able to forget she had a passenger aboard, but as soon as her step became in any way precarious she was overwhelmed with a dramatic urge for self-preservation.

The *Caliban* was a large ship with an active crew ferrying supplies back and forth, readying for departure. Juno was able to approach them without any particular ceremony; her disguise must be working, as none of them dropped their cargo to shout "Look, a duchess!"

As was common for privateers in service to Queen Aud, the crew of the *Caliban* were a brightly-coloured bunch, clad in wild finery repurposed from a previous age. Coats and corsets, silks and velvets, all ragged and sea-worn. Privateers were not pirates in any technical or legal sense, but their habits and their appearance made it clear that they knew full well most ordinary people could not tell the difference.

Perhaps a third of the crew were women, or appeared so, though they wore male trousers and jackets; most of the lace and petticoats were worn by crew members who appeared to be male.

Juno watched them for a while, admiring their industry.

Her eye was drawn to one crew member in particular: a young woman with bright blue hair piled atop her head, and a ruffled shirt worn loose over crimson breeches. She hung from an improvised rope swing in order to repaint the scratched name plate on the hull. A small paint pot hung from one elbow, and she held the brush between her teeth.

"Excuse me," Juno said politely, approaching the sailor. "Do you know where I might find.." She startled back.

The sailor blinked in recognition.

"You're…" Juno began to say. She *knew* this young lady. They'd once been part of the same bewildering house party that resolved itself into an epic magical teacup-and-cake fight, shortly followed by Juno's unexpected marriage. This was Mneme's missing cousin Metis. Henry's cousin, too. No one had set eyes on Metis Seabourne since she left for the Continent more than a year ago.

"I'm not anyone," snapped the privateer, spitting out the brush. Her Seabourne-red hair was concealed by bright blue dye, but there was no hiding her pale skin, awkwardly long neck, and freckles made all the more fierce by exposure to the sun. "What do you want, *Duchess*?" In her mouth, the title became a sneering word.

"I'm looking for J. Willoughby Bones," said Juno. "But you *are*, you know. You might as well admit it. We're cousins by marriage."

The sailor's mouth twisted up. "I suppose that's true," she said grudgingly, then tipped her head back to yell. "OI! CAPTAIN!"

The other crew members caught up her cry, and eventually Juno heard a stomp of boots on the deck.

"What's your clamour, bosun?" called a deep voice, and a shadow fell over them both.

The privateer captain of the *Caliban* was tall and

58

narrow-hipped. He wore a long leather coat over a lace shirt, and his hair hung in braids to his waist. His beard was trim, and pointed. His eyes burned into Juno as he took her in.

Another moment of recognition. This could not be a coincidence. Vance had led her here, after all, in the letter he wrote years ago.

"William," she said on a quiet breath.

"Juno," replied the man who had once been her brother-in-law. Little Will. The one who ran away from their awful family, the one who *got out*. "We should talk," he growled, gesturing with a signal to a nearby sailor, who scurried off along the deck, then scooted down the gangplank.

"She's a lady, Captain," said Metis in a quiet voice. *Lady*, of course, did not mean the same as *woman* in either of their worlds.

"Is that what she is," said William Von Trask.

"Well, you don't have to tell everyone," Juno huffed. She gave Metis an impatient look. "Don't you know a disguise when you see one?"

Metis barked out a laugh.

The sailor obeying Will's silent order finally made it to Juno's side. He gave her a quick, breathless bow and motioned that she should follow him on to the ship. As Juno complied, she felt a suspicious glare burning after her from beneath a tangle of bright blue curls.

Who would have thought this would turn into such a day of family reunions?

∾

*J*uno had never thought much of boats. She disliked the swan-shaped boats designed for the transportation of ladies, which were ugly things, deeply uncomfortable and ladened with elaborate etiquette and rituals that made them trickier to navigate than a tea party full of disapproving ladies of the peerage. Swan-shaped boats could be small transports for rivers, or larger ferries and barges for travelling between islands, but they were always ghastly. Even the spells designed to make them move along the ocean, "*as if a swan floated in calm waters*," made her sick to her stomach.

Before she rose in the ranks of the gentry, Juno had quite enjoyed the ordinary ferries between islands which were slow but satisfying, and did not require anything of you but a coin for the ferryman, and perhaps another to purchase some hot nuts for the voyage. It was easy enough to enjoy such things in the days before she was a married lady, or a duchess.

She had never spent any time around sailing ships as large as this one, though she had considered doing a Grand Tour of the Continent after Dominic sent her the funds from the sale of his father's estate. When Juno almost lost her nerve about embarking upon her first Season as a widow, she had flipped a coin: *heads*, do the Season and find a new husband; *tails*, run away to sea and eat lobsters all summer.

More recently, she and Henry had considered Continental travel as their next adventure. The thought of travelling with a husband had a delightful honeymoon air about it. Had the passenger not embarked quite so quickly, they might be sunning themselves on a foreign beach even now, eating olives and drinking wine.

Juno was also dimly aware that Mneme and Henry had

been concerned enough about Metis disappearing off the face of the earth that they were planning some kind of expedition in the near future to locate her; at least today's surprise would spare them that trouble.

Juno was led deep into the ship, past the curious eyes of the colourful crew. The captain's cabin was a large affair, a wood-lined room that filled the area from port to starboard at the very back of the ship (aft, she remembered, was the back of the ship if one were inside, and stern if one were outside — the snarky spinster sailors whose job it was to chaperone swan-shaped boats for ladies were ever so judge-mental if one got such things mixed up).

William — or Captain Bones, as he was now — had a large desk, a shelf of books, and a swinging rope hammock, with plenty of room to spare. The windows had deep ledges that might provide seating along with a few scattered chairs that suggested meetings were often held here. (Several bottles of liquor scattered around were a strong hint that perhaps those meetings were sometimes parties; either that, or the man was a drunk who did not care to hide it).

"Do you require a chaperone?" William asked as they entered the cabin — somewhat belatedly, as the two were already alone together. The damage, so to speak, was done. "I can send for Bosun Blythe to join us."

Did he mean Metis? She filed the name away to tell Henry later.

"I think I'm respectable enough for both of us," Juno said, lifting an eyebrow at him. "And happily married, actually."

He glanced at her hand, noting the lack of ring. "Hence the disguise?"

"I'm the Duchess of Storm."

He blinked. "That's a hell of a thing."

"Isn't it just?" She found herself almost laughing now. The day had turned quite absurd. "William — can I still call you that?" He had chosen an alias, after all. New names should be respected. She would be distressed to be called Mrs Von Trask now; it was hard enough to deal with a ghost who thought it appropriate to call her *wife*, or *honeybee*.

Will grinned, familiar and boyish. The William she remembered, beneath the sultry piratical costume. "If you like. My friends call me Bones. Or Captain. I don't suppose either of those fit for you and me."

"William," Juno said again. "I need your help." She reached into her second largest detachable pocket, and laid the crisp brown envelope on his wide desk.

He frowned, opened it and read the note inside.

~

***Juno, if you are reading this, I am dead.
Get out of this house, to a place of safety. Contact
JWB of the Miranda, if you need help.
Do not trust my brother.***

~

Captain Bones' face did not change as he read Vance's last message. If Juno did not know him — did not remember his bright eyes and sense of humour as a younger man — she might think him quite terrifying in this moment. A privateer captain. A killer, quite likely. Ruthless, certainly. Good with ropes, perhaps.

He blew out a breath, half-chuckling to himself. "Typical. I thought I'd got away from them all. But they knew exactly where I was, all along."

"You knew they were dead, I assume," Juno murmured. "Vance, and your father." She had never asked. William disappeared from their lives overnight, and no one ever mentioned him again.

"Dom came to find me after Father died," William said quietly. "Tried to give me blood money from the estate, like I hadn't already made my own fortune. Vance, I learned about from the newspapers back when it happened." An apology crossed his face. "I should have sent you my condolences."

"Don't worry about it on my behalf," Juno said, rolling her eyes a little.

"So odd," he said, reading the note again. "He tried to send you to me for safety. You didn't look for me then?"

"I didn't receive the letter until now. It was misplaced in a book. I saw to my own safety."

"That's Vance for you. Too smart for his own good." Will sighed, lost in thought for a moment. His gaze eventually made its way back to her. There was something warm about his presence. Perhaps the cabin itself. Far too warm. "What do you need from me now, Juno?"

"I need to find out who killed Vance, apparently. I don't suppose it was you?"

William laughed at that, though there was bitterness in it. "Coming straight out with it, I see. Is that what living with aristocrats has taught you?"

"Dukes do enjoy plain speaking."

"Do you want it to have been me?"

"It would make my life easier," she said honestly. "I don't care who did it. I just need to *know*."

"It was a hunting accident, according to reports," he shrugged. "Do you know any more than that?"

"If it's a cover story, it's the only one I was ever told."

"It could be true. He was terrible at hunting. I once

tried to teach him to use a bow and arrow, and he shot himself in the thigh. I didn't even think that was possible."

Juno tapped the letter. "And yet."

William pushed it back in her general direction. "Why is this important? You're married again. A fancy duchess. The most obvious person responsible, if it was even murder, is my father, and he's long dead. So why do you care?"

"I don't care," said Juno. "Not in the least. But…" This was the embarrassing part to say out loud. "Vance's ghost does. Care, that is."

William went quite pale. "I'm sorry," he said after a moment. "You can see *ghosts*?"

8

ROUGH SEAS MAKE GOOD
SAILORS

To Juno's surprise, William did not press for further details about his brother. Instead, he rose from his desk and led Juno back into the busy ship, heading for what turned out to be the galley — another word Juno remembered from her long and uncomfortable history with swan-shaped boats.

This tiny kitchen with its oil stove and lack of proper plumbing would have driven any cook Juno ever employed to tears. It did, however, feature substantial cupboard space with sturdy latches on every door, and a large barrel of what had to be rum.

"This is Rafferty," William said, indicating a tall, thin man with scraggly beard and an eyepatch, presiding over this sorry excuse for a kitchen. "Rafferty has been telling me for years that this galley is haunted, though the ship is barely three years old. Also, most importantly, no one has ever died here. Could you please have a look around and tell me if there's anyone here who shouldn't be?"

It was a long time since Juno had used her skills on command. "Very well," she said, since she was hoping for a favour from him in return. "What does this ghost of yours look like?"

"Oh, no one ever sees ut," Rafferty assured her. "But thungs go missung. Gut pushed off the counter when I'm not lookung. Too much salt in the stew, broken cups, that sort of thung. I tells you, we're haunted."

"Ships don't stay still, Rafferty," William growled. "If you can't keep shit from hitting the floor when the sea is rocky, you're no good to us as a cook."

"I do recommend you keep the salt somewhere other than a shelf directly over the pot," Juno agreed. "And as for the rest of the mishaps, is it possible that the cat is responsible for some of it?"

Rafferty burst into tears.

William looked about ready to stab himself. "How did you know about the bloody cat?" he groaned.

"I mean, it's right there." She pointed to the creature currently sunning himself by a sliver of sunlight coming in from the porthole.

"Can you describe it?" William asked, sounding pained.

Oh. "Tabby," Juno said, her heart sinking. "Rather unkempt, but well-fed. Shiny fur with gold flecks. One eye missing. A leg missing as well."

William let his head fall back against the door.

"Thut's my girl," sobbed Rafferty.

"And that's our mystery solved," said the captain of the *Caliban*. "Our galley is being haunted by a cat that died a year ago… and *you* can see ghosts." He met Juno's gaze steadily.

"You could have taken my word for it," she replied.

"No, I'm afraid I couldn't. You said you needed my help, Juno. I rather think I need yours, too."

*A*s they emerged on deck together, blinking in the sunlight, Metis Seabourne came up to William, pointedly ignoring the presence of Juno. "Ready to set sail, captain."

"Excellent, bosun. Loosen those ropes and we'll be on our way."

"Wait," said Juno. "You can't leave with me aboard."

William gave her an even look. "Can't I?"

She glared at him. "I'm fairly sure the Queen would look askance at an abduction."

"Not an abduction. A business arrangement." He nodded to Metis, who hesitated only a moment, and then marched back along the deck, calling out various orders that had to do with untying ropes.

"Let me off this ship," Juno hissed.

"I'm sorry," he said, not sounding sorry at all. "But I have need of your skills. And if you really are on the hopeless, pointless quest of figuring out how my brother died, then coming on this particular voyage is your most efficient way of interviewing the only remaining witness."

"You?" she challenged.

He shook his head slowly. "I was returning from the Troilish Empire during the month that Vance died. I can't imagine a person further away from the scene of the crime."

The other brother, then. Oh, gods. "Dominic," she breathed. "Really. You know where he is?"

"I can take you to where I know he's going to be."

"And how long is this voyage of yours? How dangerous is it? Where exactly are you going?"

William gave her a warm smile that, for a less irritated woman than herself, might have been melting. "A few hours to get there. The same to get home. Minimal danger while on the actual ship, unless you fall overboard. And as for where we are going, it's an island you have probably never heard of. It does not exist on any map. The only way to get there is by ship."

The ship creaked beneath them. The sails unfurled. They really were leaving.

Juno had a choice in that moment. Not much of one, as she felt her former brother-in-law would not hesitate to restrain her if he was so set on her joining this brief voyage. But, still. She was a duchess. If she made enough of a fuss, she could probably get off this ship.

But then it would be at least seven days before her ring could be repaired, and who knew what damage the previous duchess could do to their house in that time. Getting the transient vapour to Gundrow's had to be Juno's first responsibility. She did not know how long Henry would be gone, and she could not bear the thought of him returning to Storm North in its current state of chaos — she had been left in charge, after all…

"I will go with you," she said finally. "But I have further questions."

"Ask them later." Captain Bones strode away from her, his boots ringing against the planks, and leaped up to the quarter deck. "Gentle ruffians!" he declared. The whole crew stopped what they were doing to watch him. "We have a guest on board. Treat her with all the kindness and civility you have at your disposal. She is a relative of mine." He blew Juno a kiss.

She rolled her eyes at him.

"What kind of relative, captain?" asked one of the gentle ruffians, a cheeky-eyed fellow with a torn petticoat worn over his breeches, and bright purple ribbons braided into his beard. "Didn't know you had a sister."

William met Juno's eyes for a moment. "Sister-in-law," he announced, causing quite a whispered commotion among the crew. "You will address the lady as the Widow Bones. My dear Juno," he added, in a less shouty voice. "Make yourself at home in my cabin. The rest of us have work to do."

~

There was nothing uncomfortable about the captain's spacious cabin. Juno nevertheless found herself quite unsettled. She could only sit for short amounts of time before the passenger demanded she stand up. The tilting of the ship back and forth made her as uneasy on her feet as those awful swan-shaped boats always had, in the dark days before ladies were allowed to travel by portal.

She wanted tea. She wanted her own bed, and her husband by her side. She wanted her friends clustered around her. Spoiled as she had become over the last few years, she wanted her *maid*.

Instead, she had a ship full of wildly-costumed privateers, and a former brother-in-law who apparently had better things to do than discuss why, in fact, he was so interested in ghosts.

She was bored and lonely. It was almost enough to make her take out that letter and command Vance to keep her company.

Almost. She would regret it, she knew, if she spoke the words aloud.

Still, it was enormous relief when someone came to bring her refreshment, a few hours into their voyage; a familiar face was a familiar face, however unfriendly.

Metis Seabourne, AKA Bosun Blythe, pushed her way

into the cabin, carrying the most grudging tray of sand-wiches Juno had ever seen in her life. "Why are you here?" the girl burst out, as she banged the tray down upon the desk.

"Ask your captain," Juno replied. "It was not *my* idea to bring me along for the ride like a spare piece of luggage."

"A duchess does not belong on this ship."

"Neither does a lady, come to that."

Metis looked horrified. "Don't call me that. I'm not a Lady anything. Not even an Honourable."

"We met at a garden party, *Miss* Metis Seabourne. What am I supposed to call you?"

The blue-haired girl turned on her fiercely. "My name is Blythe, privateer in the Queen's navy. I worked my way up from deckhand to bosun in less than a year. I am *good* at this life, and I will not have you or your bloody husband trying to rescue me away from it." She had clearly been practicing her sailor swearing in her time on board ship; Juno, who liked to practice a little sailor swearing herself from time to time, admired how easily she did it.

"Well, who offered?" Juno replied. "I'm not here to rescue anyone. You seem fine. What does a bosun do, anyway?"

Metis huffed at her. "It's short for boatswain. I care for the ship and its equipment. Keep the gear in good shape. Mind the hull. Supervise the crew on deck.

"That all sounds very senior."

"It is! It's a lot of responsibility, and I am excellent at it."

"Did you expect me to disapprove?" Juno shook her head. "It all seems jolly good, Metis. As long as you're happy, then Henry will be delighted."

Metis scowled at her. "I don't care if you disapprove or not. You're going to tell Henry?"

"Of course I am. I wouldn't keep this from him, or Mneme. They've been worried sick. But no one will come and rescue you unless you actually require rescuing."

"I don't."

"Fine."

"Fine!"

"So," Juno continued smoothly. "Now we have established that you are exactly where you should be, perhaps you could answer a question or two of mine?"

"I won't betray any of the captain's secrets," Metis said staunchly, folding her arms.

"Who asked you to? I'm sure Will would answer my questions himself if he weren't so very busy up on deck. We are related, after all."

Metis silently mouthed the name 'Will' to herself. "I thought that was a lie," she muttered. "A cover story. Are you really the Widow Bones?" She frowned, thinking it through. "No. That wasn't your name when you started the Season, was it. You were Mrs—"

"Careful," Juno said gently. "I won't betray your captain's secrets any more than yours. He might not have realised you could put all that together when he claimed me."

"I won't tell anyone," Metis breathed, but Juno could see her mentally file the name 'Von Trask' to think over later.

Best to move on while they were as close as they might ever be to being friendly with each other. "Where are we going?" Juno asked. "Captain Bones said it had something to do with ghosts."

"I mean," Metis shrugged. "It's called Ghost Island, but that's just a name. No actual ghosts that I know about."

Well, most people didn't see them. Though Metis was a Seabourne, so anything was possible.

"Ghost Island," Juno considered thoughtfully. "It's less than a day's journey?"

"Of course. We'll be there by teatime. Have to be, really, as we're bringing the tea."

"I'm sorry?"

Metis winced. "It's a bit embarrassing, really. Mostly our job is more exciting than this. Privateer vessels are like pirate ships, but on behalf of the Queen. We pull raids, gather information. It's half spying, half making mayhem. Little cake deliveries are not our usual line of work."

"Little cake deliveries. Is that a metaphor?"

"No," Metis sighed. "We are literally delivering little cakes. Ghost Island is off the map, right? It's small, unassuming. You can't get there by portal, and you can't find it unless you know exactly where it is. So people have been using it for centuries for meetings that never happened. Secret diplomacy. And I guess, luring people to ambushes. Right now, there's a big secret gathering happening on Ghost Island. We don't get to know details, but it goes all the way to the top. Something royal. Otherwise, the captain would have told us more about it. He's good like that."

Oh, no. Juno had a bad feeling about this. "A secret meeting of high significance, happening on an island that doesn't officially exist," she murmured. Henry was going to kill her. 'Something royal' more than likely meant that *he* was on that island, taking part in whatever secret diplomacy was happening. Mneme and Thornbury, too.

Juno had promised she would stay home. There was no way they would believe she had crashed their mission by accident.

"We're delivering the tea and cakes," Metis said, like

this was the worst thing that had ever happened to her. "We're supposed to be lions of the sea. Not blooming caterers."

Lions of the sea. It sounded like an exciting life.

"Why did you do this?" Juno blurted out. "Why leave your whole family behind to be a privateer?"

There had been a family scandal, of course; Metis' mamma was still imprisoned in the Tower for her crimes.

"Why does anyone leave one life for another?" said Metis morosely. "It was an accident, mostly. Best accident I ever had."

"And he's good to you, Will… Captain Bones? He's a good captain?" Another person who had reinvented himself, abandoning one life for another. Juno had great sympathy. She adored her current life, but it had taken her a long time to find it. And in truth, it had mostly been accidental, too. A stroke of luck. A question asked at the right moment.

"He's the best," Metis said fiercely.

Yes, Juno had always thought so. Of all the Von Trasks, William was the least worst. She hoped it was true. That he, at least, had not murdered his brother.

Or at least, that he was honourable enough to admit it if he had, so she could wash her hands of this whole dead husband business one way or another.

"You still haven't told me what brings you here," said Metis. "Ghosts?"

"Your aunt is haunting my house," Juno sighed. "It's rather a long story."

Metis looked horrified. "My aunt? Which one?"

"The dead one."

"Antiope. Oh, bad luck. She's a *lot*."

"You're telling me! She does not approve of the new Duchess of Storm at all."

"She never approved much of me, either," said Metis. "None of them thought I was ever going to amount to much." She looked glum, obviously thinking of her lack of success on the marriage market.

"You showed them," said Juno, with complete sincerity.

Metis gave her a slow grin. "Didn't I."

9

STORM WARNING

"*L*and ho!"

They came in sight of the island well before tea time.

The afternoon sun, peeking out from behind the gathering clouds, was warm on Juno's face as she walked on deck, with Metis trailing behind her. Boldly, she stepped directly up on to the quarter deck to stand beside the captain.

William — Captain Bones — leaned against the wheel, his eyes to the island as it grew on the horizon. There were other ships dotted around the coast, many of them draped with bright colours.

Oh, Juno realised, as she took in the flags, coats of arms, and other displays of identity arrayed upon the ships. Not only a royal summit. An *international* summit. The Queen must be using this secret island for some kind of covert meeting with representatives of other countries.

The countries of Arunia, Gedos and Treventral, based on the flags Juno could see. When she was first let in on the secret of her husband's more covert adventures in diplomacy and espionage, she had spent several weeks doing deep research on Continental politics.

A momentary twinge of jealousy overtook her. As the wife of the Duke of Storm, whose public support for the Queen was well known, Juno should have been part of all this. Secretive political meetings were boring and pointless, but royal affairs where the politics happened during ceremonies with teacups and cake were exactly the sort of affair to which you which *you brought your wife*.

Juno was nearly six months pregnant and perfectly well. There was no need to retire her to a swooning couch just yet.

"I don't need you yet, your grace," the captain said in an undertone as she moved to his side.

"You quite surprise me," she said calmly. "Sailing a peer of the realm across the ocean, for no particular reason. Did you think I had nothing better to do today?"

He gave her a long look. "Perhaps you would care to join us on the island, Widow Bones?"

"What a lovely idea. I would enjoy the chance to stretch my legs. Do not expect me to fetch and carry."

"I wouldn't dare," he replied, with an expression that might have been amusement.

"And this purpose you may or may not have for my particular skillset," she went on. "Will it be helped or hindered by the certainty that some of the people meeting on that island will recognise me?"

William froze. "Ah."

"You forgot," she said, almost amused.

"In my defence, you weren't a duchess the last time we spent any amount of time together."

"It's still rather embarrassing for you. I don't suppose you have a list of attendees I could run my eye over? To be sure of avoiding awkward reunions?"

"I don't need one," he said, wincing. "I know who's at the top of the list."

Juno conveyed her impatience with a look. "Let me guess," she said, keeping her tone barely above whisper. "Her majesty. Lord Manticore, he's rarely far from her side. Not to mention the Duke of Storm, his cousin Mrs Seabourne, and *her* husband. Plus the usual hordes of elderly aunties and ladies-in-waiting who have spent the last year turning their nose up at me in court, and therefore know exactly what I look like. Am I close?"

William was beginning to look rather annoyed. "Did you know about this summit all along?"

"I worked it out when your bosun brought me sandwiches. Which were dry, by the way. I hope the refreshments you are bringing for the Queen are in better condition." Juno put her hands on her hips, facing William down with the imperious scorn she had been honing since she first became a duchess. "You brought me all this way. Don't you think it's time you told me why?"

The privateer captain tilted his head at her with a thoughtful glower that reminded her he was not just her youngest former brother-in-law. Privateers were a law unto themselves, and she imagined that went double for their captains. "How are you at illusion charms?" he asked.

"How good to I need to be to fool my husband, do you think?" she retorted. As it happened, Juno was very good at illusion charms; they were the kind of small magic at which she excelled. But William did not need to know that yet. "Where are the ghosts, Captain Bones?" she pressed.

"That's what I need you to tell me," he burst out impatiently.

Ghost Island was getting closer. It seemed perfectly pleasant: no ominous skull-shaped rocks or wraith-like trees. Nothing at all to earn it a name associated with the spirit world.

"Perhaps I should ask my husband," Juno said in frustration, flinging up her arms and marching to the railing. "Since he's right there."

"No, wait—"

His look of alarm was priceless. Juno stepped away from the edge. "I was making a point. Did you think I was going to jump into the sea? I don't plan to go down in history as the first Duchess of Storm to be drowned by heavy layers of wet taffeta."

"Could you just—" William sighed. "Could you stop being dramatic long enough for me to explain?"

"Let's find out."

He took a deep breath. "Her majesty's intelligence service have uncovered a plot to kill one of the delegates. The rumour is that the assassin has been working across the Continent for some time."

"That sounds alarming."

"They call him the Ghost. Some say he returned from the dead; others call him unkillable. He's murdered men in locked rooms, in impossible situations. Disappeared like smoke. All I need is for you to do is to stay at my side, don't get recognised, keep an eye out, and tell me if you see anyone I don't."

Juno frowned at him. "You think this assassin is a literal ghost?"

"I'd like to have confirmation he is not." He scowled. "I have my suspicions."

"This is a lot of highly sensitive information for a cake delivery person. Who are you really, William?"

His handsome face closed over. He looked as distant and dangerous as the first time she had seen him leaning over the hull of his ship.

"I'm the Queen's man," he said flatly. "That is all you need to know."

Juno sighed heavily. The Queen's man. As if she needed another one of those in her life.

~

The Widow Bones went ashore on Ghost Island along with the captain, the bosun, and several members of the crew of the *Caliban*. Thanks to a discreet facial illusion charm, tethered to an exceedingly respectable lace bonnet, she did not look even slightly like Juno Jupiter, Duchess of Storm.

No one asked her to assist in the carrying of crates. She was not sure if that was because she had reached the point of her delicate condition when it was extremely obvious, even beneath bunches of ghoulishly black taffeta, or simply out of respect for the fact that she was aboard as a member of the captain's family.

There were several shade pavilions set up on the sands, but there was nothing about them that screamed royalty. Juno was therefore not surprised when their little caravan of cakes continued up a sandy path, and into the trees.

They walked for some time before emerging into a clearing by a waterfall. A Very Royal Indeed pavilion had been set up on a grassy mound, with a few plain tents behind, probably for servants and storage. Keeping close to Metis, Juno observed some familiar figures lounging on cushioned seating.

Queen Aud was adorned in so many pearl filigree brooches that she was at serious risk of being carried away by a passing raven. She wore a violet bonnet and matching gown in such light layers of fabric, you might think the picnic was planned for spring time instead of the dead of autumn. Her dark, curly hair was coiled tightly in a formal arrangement that must have taken days to perfect. She looked, as always, lovely.

Standing at her back was Alfred Lord Manticore, Queen's Advisor on Magical Matters (and, it was rumoured since his hasty recent divorce, her paramour). A tall, handsome and glowering man, he looked, as usual, like he would like very much to strike everyone with lightning bolts from his fingers.

Lady Ashby, Countess Phyllida of Glass… goodness, half the court was here: the elderly female half who could claim some kind of kinship to the Queen. Good luck to them all keeping this assignation secret, with so many of the Isle of Town's most notorious gossips in attendance.

More and more, it was starting to look like this was not a summit of political significance, and was instead a party from which the Duchess of Storm had been deliberately excluded.

Given how many times she had been sneered at or quietly mocked for marrying so far above her station by these particular prissed-up snootbuckets, it was hard not to feel rejected.

~

The Chamberlain of the Court waited for the delivery from the *Caliban* behind the plain tents, receiving their crates of supplies with a mixture of relief and impatience. "I trust the ice has not melted?"

"I mean, it's ice," said Captain Bones with a rakish grin that only added to his disreputable, leather-clad appearance. "One can only fight the tide for so long."

The crew of the *Caliban*, clearly not interested in party management, tried to set the crates down any old where, without a sense of order or reason. Juno watched them do it for about thirty seconds before she began to instruct them in how to arrange the supplies in proper order: the cold crates to one side, and the crates shimmering with preservation spells to the other, separate from those that contained tableware, including the porcelain cups and saucers.

"Don't throw that one down," she cautioned at one point. "Just because it says cake forks on the outside is no reason to be sloppy."

"Yes ma'am," said the sailor, then looked horrified at himself. "I mean…"

"My sister speaks with my voice, Hobsbawn," growled Captain Bones. He sounded fierce but had a twinkle in his eye.

"Yes cap'n," said the sailor, setting down the crate of cake forks with surprising delicacy, before fleeing the tent.

Juno herself left the tent a few moments later. It was warm in the kitchen tent, and it didn't do to call attention to herself by swooning or any such rot. A small breath of fresh air was all she needed to revive herself.

She took three steps away from the entry flap, and came face to face with her husband.

Henry looked wonderful.

Well, he looked as he always did — large and open-faced, terribly handsome, with a cravat that somehow loosened itself the second he was more than five minutes away from his valet. (Was Mr Marlborough on one of those ships in the bay, Juno had to wonder?)

He was close enough for her to know that he smelled like sand, and his own soap, and *Henry*. She wanted to kiss his throat. Wanted to throw herself into his arms and declare that the management of his dead mother was entirely his problem.

Gods, she wanted a nap.

Henry, Duke of Storm, smiled politely at her with a complete lack of recognition.

Score one for the illusion charm, score minus seventy-three for wedded bliss.

"Excuse me, madam," he asked politely. "Have the crew of the *Caliban* arrived?"

A new thought, crashing in on her: where was Metis right now? They had walked together at one point. Was the ship's bosun in the tent, or already heading back to the ship for more supplies? It would be a dreadful distraction for Henry to be confronted with his long-lost cousin in the middle of whatever precious walk-on-eggshells diplomacy was being wrought here.

Juno could not speak for a moment, frozen in second-hand anxiety. And then, out of the corner of her eye, she saw a coiled mass of blue hair come around the corner of the tents. Metis was with another crew member, carrying a case of ratafia between them, conversing in quiet voices.

Juno stepped aside, drawing Henry's eye, and then indicated the opening of the tent with a flourish.

"Thank you so much," he said graciously, and ducked inside.

Juno let out a swallow of air that had almost choked her. Why hadn't she just — told him —

Metis, a few feet away, had caught sight of the exchange and was pale beneath her freckles like she had seen a ghost.

"What, I have to carry it in myself?" protested the other crew member.

"Sorry, I have to help the captain's sister," said Metis, releasing her side of the case. She grabbed Juno's arm, and the two of them hurried off into the trees together.

"I think I'm going to be sick," said Juno, clutching at the nearest sturdy tree trunk.

"Why is he here?" wailed Metis.

Belatedly it occurred to Juno that Metis had no idea of her cousin's vocation. She must have no idea he had spent most of his adult life throwing himself into peril for the sake of queen, country and the Teacup Isles.

"It's a party," she said, recovering her own sensibilities as quickly as she could. "Queen Aud is here. You know what a social butterfly Henry is."

"It's not just a party though, is it?" Metis' eyes narrowed. "What do you know?"

Juno felt as if her heart was going to explode. Why was this dress so uncomfortably tight when it was constructed from so much dashed fabric? "Give me a minute," she pleaded.

Large, hot arms came around her, grabbing her roughly. A hand, smelling oddly of nothing, covered her face. For one horrible moment, she could not breathe at all. As her vision blurred, Juno saw Metis draw a short sword, her face alight with fury...

And then darkness, only darkness.

Before Juno went under completely, she heard a dead man's voice say the words: "I'd also like to know, Widow Bones. Why is the Duke of Storm here on this island?"

She recognised that voice. She had hoped very much never to hear that voice again.

10

NICE DAY FOR A FAILED WEDDING

*I*t had not exactly been the world's most romantic proposal.

Juno and so many other eligible ladies treated the entire house party as a game: counting how many minutes they might keep the Duke in conversation, or how many laughs one might provoke from him at supper.

They used magics — small, sympathetic charms for the most part — to soften his heart towards them, and to counteract each other's enchantments.

It was silly, and it was fun, and somewhere along the way, Juno discovered that she was rather good at it all.

What else might I be good at? she wondered.

Then, the rules changed. Henry was abducted. Juno and her new friends — the horde of ladies in line for the Duke's hand — teamed up with his cousins Mneme and Metis to save him from a forced marriage. To his *aunt*, of all people!

When it was all over, every enchantment was broken (along with several dozen teacups), Henry, Duke of Storm, sat alone on a wrought iron bench in the garden of Shell-wich Standing, looking utterly wrecked.

He was covered in cake, spilled tea, and all manner of odd substances leftover from the spells that had flown wildly through the air in the temple. Were those marigold petals sticking to his sleeve, thanks to a large smear of whipped cream?

Oh, he was a tragic sight. Shoulders slumped. Eyes downcast. Misery was smeared across his face, like butter on toast.

Mneme and her mother and the servants rushed around trying to see to their confused guests. The guilty party had been taken away by royal agents, in collaboration with the local constabulary.

Most of the ladies were now laughing and sharing tea, shaking off the oddness of the day.

No one had thought to comfort Henry, or even to converse with him. At first, he was engaged by the magisters and spellcrackers whose job it was to ensure his mind was free of enchantments, but now…

Now, in this moment, he sat alone on a bench.

Juno made a choice.

"Well!" she announced as she sat beside him, not caring if her gown got smeared by the cream and cake crumbs that adorned his own wedding finery. "I do look forward to reading the society pages this week. How will they manage to convince anyone they're telling the truth?"

The Duke gave her a weary smile. Warm eyes, she thought. A decent sort of person, despite all this wealth, privilege and his usual boisterous personality. "I can't quite believe it myself," he said. "This is not how I thought my house party would turn out."

"Do house parties among the peerage not usually end

with abductions and tea fights?" she asked mockingly. "Aren't we the lucky ones?"

His smile faltered a little, as if he was not quite ready to make light of it all, not yet. "My *aunt*," he said in a choked voice.

"Yes, well," said Juno with an airy wave of her hand. "Everyone has odd skeletons in their family history. Yours is merely…"

"More embarrassing than most."

"Only today. By tomorrow someone's great-uncle will have nominated a horse to Parliament, and it will all be forgotten."

The Duke sighed, leaning back into the bench and wriggling his feet as if he'd quite like to be out of his boots. For a moment Juno had a vision of him in a dressing gown and slippers, and then cast it out of her mind as entirely presumptuous.

"The worst part of it is," he muttered. "I still have to get married. I promised my mother on her deathbed, and I've left it all far too late. There must be a new Duchess of Storm."

Juno could do the polite, demurring thing at this point. But why? It had been a long day. Perhaps, for once in her life, she could let herself be presumptuous.

"Easily resolved," she said cheerfully. "Marry me."

She wasn't thinking through all the ramifications of *what it would be like to be the Duchess of Storm*, not really. She was thinking that he had warm eyes, and she'd never seen him be cruel to anyone, though he was constantly surrounded by dull people wanting his attention.

There was a solidity to him that she liked. A sense of humour. It was a dizzying thought, that marriage might be a place where laughter belonged. For a moment, she actually let herself want something, very badly.

He was everything, *everything* she had not found in her first husband.

Henry looked amused. She couldn't tell if he was taking her seriously. "Just like that, Mrs Von Trask?"

"Just like that," she replied with an assurance she almost felt. "You like me, I like you. We'd rub along rather nicely. We're not related in the least — *cousin* is almost as bad as aunt in my book, best avoided — and I've only ever attempted to put the tiniest, most insignificant magical spells on you, in a social situation where it is practically expected. I promise never to do such a thing again, if you wish."

After the events of the day, it was possible he might be rather sensitive about being enchanted. Juno was more than willing to respect that particular boundary. She had rather lost the taste for love spells after seeing the tableau in the temple.

"All right," said the Duke of Storm, unexpectedly.

"What?"

"Let's get married."

She burst into laughter. "Really?"

"Why not?" He looked rather merry, his eyes sparkling. Then he took a deep breath. "Making decisions feels marvellous. Like someone just lifted a house off my shoulders."

Juno herself felt untethered. Reality had suddenly shifted beneath her feet. "Luckily for you, I'm excellent at making decisions for other people."

"Can it be a small wedding?" He was practically glowing in the sunshine.

"The smallest," she agreed, feeling quite giddy about the whole thing.

"And not here." He gestured around at the chaos of the manor garden.

"Definitely not here."

"Do you have a dress? I mean, that dress is lovely…"

"Henry," Juno said, laughing, because damned if she wasn't going to call him by his first name. "It doesn't have to be this very minute. You might like to bathe first. Make a few plans."

His expression, if it were at all possible, became even warmer. "Soon, though," he insisted.

"Yes," she said, smiling wildly. "As soon as you like."

He leaped to his feet. "I must tell Aunt Galatea. That's the aunt who wasn't arrested. And Mneme!"

"You might inform your Mr Thornbury as well," Juno said, amused at his energy. "He'll want to thoroughly check you over and assure himself I have not cast a spell on you."

Henry, Duke of Storm, gave her a blazing smile that heated her all the way to her bones. "You rather have, you know."

Then he took off, running across the grass, avoiding the debris of broken teacups. "Mnemo! Guess what?"

11

FINE WEATHER FOR GHOSTS

When Juno awoke, she found herself surrounded by the dead.

These were old ghosts; hauntings that had been tethered to the mortal realm for decades, possibly centuries.

Juno lay on a clifftop, with a magnificent view of the bright blue ocean. Not a ship in sight, so they must be further around the coast from the bay where the Queen and her navy were moored.

The ghosts were all around her. Some sprawled on the sandy rock. Others drifted back and forth. A lady in thick, layered petticoats and a bodice two centuries out of fashion fell, screaming silently, over the edge of the cliff only to reappear moments later, blinking in the sunshine. After staring in confusion at her surroundings for a moment, she took two steps and fell again…

Juno ripped her eyes away from the sight. There were skeletons here; rough sun-bleached bones scattered around the rocks. People had died in this place and no one had ever stopped to bury their bodies.

She turned again, towards a scent of smoke and tea.

A man in black sat beside a campfire, boiling a billy-can. "Your grace," he said in a polite, deadpan voice.

"You're still alive, then," she said in return. Which was nonsensical, now she came to think of it, but she was owed a little nonsense.

The faces of the dead loomed around the man in black. Were they tethered to this place, this killing ground… or to him?

People weren't supposed to be haunted, Juno reminded herself. *Places* could be haunted. Objects… not people. She had done extensive reading on the subject. She should know.

This man in black, he was no ghost, though there were similarities to a ghost she had spoken to quite recently.

Dominic Von Trask was taller than Vance, not quite as tall as William. His shoulders wider than either of them. He held himself still, with more physical restraint than his brothers. Which made sense, because he was far more dangerous.

His hands glittered with silver rings; one in particular was a spiral of skulls that hummed with magical power.

His voice had sent chills through her in that moment before she lost consciousness. It was so similar to the voice of his father and she knew, she was *certain* that man was dead. She would never feel truly safe if it were otherwise.

Dominic had none of Will's warmth; none of Vance's charm. If one only considered the cheekbones and the shape of his jaw, he was better looking than either of them, and yet Juno had never found him particularly attractive.

Like his father before him, Dominic Von Trask had the ability to terrify simply by making eye contact. The family fixer. He could talk anyone into the deal he most wanted, because everyone was afraid what he might do if they said no.

Juno had never been put in a position of having to say no to Dominic, except for that last day when she made it clear to him that she would leave the house, leave the family, forever. (She knew she only got away with her flight because he allowed it. He did not want to marry his brother's widow any more than she wanted him.)

Slowly now, Juno sat up. She could avoid looking directly at the surrounding ghosts if she concentrated on the man she had known years ago. Had called brother, if with a certain degree of discomfort. "Hello, Dominic," she said in a civilised tone of voice.

The whole cliffside crackled with magic: dark magic. *His* magic. It was not only the presence of so many ghosts around them that made Juno think of shadows, and of death. She had met many magisters in her time, those wielders of power who had more than everyday magic flowing in their veins. Those who had educated, shaped, tailored their magic into something mighty and earth-shattering.

She had never been this close to a necromancer before, one whose magic was grounded in death, and yet she had no doubt that was what she was looking at. Dominic's magical education had taken him down a particularly dark path.

Why was he here? (William had promised to give Juno a chance to talk with him, had he not? How had William possibly known that Dominic would end up here, of all places, on an island that did not appear on any map, during a gathering of such high royal importance and secrecy?)

"Oh," she said with a small huff of surprise, remembering everything else William had said about this island, this mission. "Of course. *You're* the Ghost."

(Brother-in-law most likely to grow up to be a magical

assassin… take a bow, Juno, you're full of all the answers today.)

Dominic smiled sharply at her. "I knew you were smart," he said, like he'd won something. "My father underestimated you."

"Who are you here to kill?" she asked immediately. If she was going to suffer the embarrassment of being kidnapped, she might as well try to dig some useful information out of him. William had warned of a plot to kill one of the delegates…

"Your husband, apparently," Dominic replied without an ounce of shame.

Perhaps Juno was still a bit light-headed from whatever he had used to knock her out, but her immediate response was: "What, again?"

His face darkened. "What's that supposed to mean?"

She should be cautious. Juno knew that. This man had been dangerous enough when they lived in the same house, and he had clearly spent the last few years approaching a whole new level of sinister.

But she was tired and irritated, and *kidnapped*, and she wasn't very happy about the whole Henry situation, and when she looked at Dominic she saw 'worst brother-in-law in the land' before she saw 'person who could kill me right now on the spot and walk away smiling.'

"Vance," she said, to see if there might be a hint of guilt in his expression. No. Dominic Von Trask might as well be carved out of the same granite as this cliff.

"What about Vance?" he asked.

"He's under the impression that you murdered him."

For one second, she actually thought she might have shocked him. Then the magical assassin known as the Ghost threw back his head and laughed. "Oh, of *course* you talk to the spirit world," he said. "That's the cherry on the cake. How long has my fool of a brother been haunting you?"

"Two days, which is quite enough, thank you very much," Juno said tartly.

"Lucky you," Dominic replied. "He's been haunting me for years." He pulled a watch on a chain out of his waistcoat and held it up. "I never knew he was so sentimental, but it turns out he has an attachment to old detritus."

"That *rat*," Juno said, fury welling up. She rummaged through her pockets, running her fingers briefly over the tiny velvet-wrapped glass vial that had miraculously remained unbroken, and finally the letter, which she flourished in the air. "Vance Von Trask, show yourself!"

There was a shiver in the air as something ineffable was displaced, and then her former husband appeared: one more spirit among the ghouls and the skeletons. Vance crossed gingerly towards his brother, brushing imaginary dust from his sleeves. "Hell of a destination you've chosen for this particular reunion, honey bee."

"You've been haunting Dominic all this time?" Juno accused. "If you have a pet assassin at your disposal, what was the point of dragging me along on your wild goose chase?"

"I haunt everyone," Vance said sullenly. "There isn't a lot else to do. Not that I ever made much progress with Will. He's got less Sight than your average house brick, and there's a cat on that ship that *does not* like me."

The passenger turned somersaults inside Juno; they were both equally uncomfortable with all this standing around. Possibly there needed to be a nap in their near future: one not induced by strange potions or magics. Oh, gods, what had Dominic dosed her with? Was it harmful for babies?

"Well?" she demanded, more snappishly than she might have before she had that thought about sleeping potions. "I don't imagine you need a chaperone for this conversation."

Vance and Dominic looked at her, equally blank.

She gestured impatiently at them both. "This one wants to know how he died. You're a witness. Put him out of his misery so he can put me out of mine."

"He won't say," Vance grumbled. "You think I haven't asked? He likes to watch me suffer. I thought he'd tell you," he added sullenly. "He likes you more than me."

"That isn't hard," said Dominic coldly. "I hate to tell you, dear brother, but I know no more than you do. I'm not the witness you're looking for."

"That can't be true," said Juno. "You left together on that hunting trip. Vance did not come back alive. Surely you know *something*." Dominic had looked grim enough, on the day he and Bertram returned to the house to announce she was a widow. The thought that he did not know what happened made no sense at all.

"I know many things," said Dominic. "But I did not see my brother die."

"That's not an answer."

He began to say something in return, then held up a hand. "Someone's coming."

"Speaking as your current kidnap victim, I do hope so," Juno grumbled.

He shook his head at her. "You're really not scared of me."

"That depends."

"On what?"

"On whether or not you plan to kill the husband I actually *like*."

"Ouch," said Vance, but no one was listening to him at all.

~

*I*t was a messy rescue attempt. Henry and Thornbury came at them from one side, Will and his privateers from the other. There was a moment when Juno realised she was still nearer to Dominic than any of them: he could easily reach out and kill her if he wished. For both of their sakes she was glad he did not.

There was a magical net, a cloud of enchanted sleep-steam, and a wild-eyed, blue-haired bosun wielding a knife. At one point, Thornbury stepped directly into Dominic's path, and Juno felt her heart in her throat, knowing her friend's happiness depended on that wretched spellcracker staying alive…

Dominic's eyes met hers, briefly, and then he vanished into shadows as if he had never been there.

"What the hell kind of magic was that?" Thornbury demanded, throwing his arms up in frustration.

Juno didn't care. They were all alive, and Henry was there in front of her, *did she mention alive*, catching her up in his arms…

Later, she would be infuriated that Dominic managed somehow to evade them all without answering any of the questions she had asked. The only 'ghost' she wanted to talk to, and he was nowhere to be found…

And, presumably, he still had designs to make her a widow for the second time.

She was going to have to do something about him.

12

RIGHT AS RAIN

"*T*rather like you in black," said Henry, some hours later.

The mysterious tea party involving the Queen and the delegates from the Continental countries of Arunia, Gedos and Trevental had been postponed to the following day after the Interruption By Assassin. A breakfast was planned instead.

One could only hope that the crates of supplies brought in on the *Caliban* had been placed under the sturdiest of preservation spells, and that their visitors from the Continent did not object to consuming cakes and tiny sandwiches for breakfast.

Thornbury and several other agents of the Crown, along with their general cohort of guards and magisters, were combing the island for the Ghost, without any apparent understanding of irony.

To Henry's deep frustration, he had now been grounded — or shipped, thanks to his official role as Delegate Under Threat. He and Juno were sequestered in the rather luxurious stateroom in Lord Manticore's own flagship, the *Bonny Elk*, while Lord Manticore himself led the protection detail for the Queen and her ladies (including Mneme Seabourne) over in the *Majestic Harvest*.

After so much fussing on land, and being reunited with her husband under such drastic and crowded circumstances, Juno had been longing for some privacy. However, as soon as the door closed on the stateroom, leaving them alone together for the first time in days, she realised that there were many conversations that Needed To Be Had between Henry and herself, and she did not have the faintest idea where to begin.

The colour of her gown, apparently, was the conversational opening he chose.

"It washes me out," she sighed, making herself as comfortable as she could on a couch that had not been designed for any civilised drawing room. "I must look a sight."

"At least it's your face, and not that illusion charm you hoped to fool me with earlier," said her husband.

She did not know what she had expected; surely not a blazing row, which was not their style at all. But she had not thought he would be so calm about suddenly finding her (and the passenger, of course, heir to the title, blah blah blah) on a dangerous island, caught up in everything he had tried to protect her from.

"You didn't recognise me," she said, matching his tone: lighthearted and a little flirtatious. "Admit it. You looked right through me."

"It took me a few seconds to make the connection," he admitted. "I've never seen you wear that particular gown. And your illusion charms are devastatingly good. But, Juno, don't think for a moment you escaped my notice."

That at least was worthy of a kiss, and she could not think of a nicer way to distract them both from the oncoming storm of politics and death threats about to crash around them. She reached her arms up in invitation and Henry came to her, leaning over her on the couch for a most overdue embrace.

This, she had missed. They had only been apart a few days, and yet so much had happened.

"Tell me about how you apparently have a whole other life of conversing with ghosts," he murmured into her throat. "I can't believe I never knew."

"I didn't want to tell you," she sighed. "We barely knew each other when we married, and once that ring of yours stopped it all, I felt as if a curse had been lifted. Saying it out loud might bring it all back."

"Ah yes, the family ring. At Gundrow's, I hope?" Henry kissed her finger, where Juno missed the heaviness of the jewelled band.

"Safe and sound. But unfortunately, it requires a unique ingredient." Quickly, she explained the matter of the transient vapour, and how she had rather hoped that her first husband's entirely un-mysterious murder might be the quickest route to acquire such a substance.

"You know, my dear, our family has had an account at Gundrow's for centuries," said Henry. "Providing the ingredients comes under the heading of full service."

"The matter had become rather urgent," Juno said tartly. "I did not wish to wait around for whatever random ghost-seeing messengers our jeweller was able to employ."

Henry's jaw became somewhat belligerent. "Urgent enough to risk sailing into the unknown and getting yourself kidnapped by an infamous assassin?"

Risking herself *and* the passenger; he had not spoken that particular reproof aloud, but she heard it all the same.

"That all just sort of happened," she said impatiently.

"You can't keep me in a museum case, Henry. I found Metis for you, didn't I?"

"Oh, yes, wasn't that a shock — my sweet youngest cousin, now a wild blue-haired pirate leaping upon me in a forest to let me know my wife had been kidnapped by an assassin. What a hoyden she has become."

"I think her new life suits her," Juno said primly.

"That's hardly the point. Which was, in case you don't know that *I* know how you were trying to distract me, that *you*, my love, should not be anywhere near this island."

"That wasn't my idea. That was her majesty's own privateer captain."

"Your other brother-in-law. Oh, what a tangled web we weave."

"And besides," Juno said, grumpy at being chided. "Our home was no longer any kind of safe haven. Believe me, I'm in less danger here."

His ears pricked up. "What do you mean by that?"

Ah. There was no easy way to say this next part. "In the absence of the family ring, Storm North has become somewhat haunted." *Infested* might be a better word. "The ghost in question is the most powerful and affecting I have ever known. I had to close the house up and send all the servants away for their safety."

"Oh dear." Henry's tone changed, becoming somewhat apologetic. "It's true, there are some bad eggs on the family tree. Was it one of the old dukes? Hopefully not the one with all the dead wives."

"How many dead wives?" A certain number was not unusual in any ancestor; it had to be a truly alarming quantity to be worthy of note.

Henry nodded grimly. "They had to embroider a whole separate panel for the Jupiter tapestry, just to fit them all in. One of my Great Grandmammas turned it into a throw cushion in the hopes of hiding the family shame."

"It wasn't a duke," Juno told him.

"A duchess, then? Or one of the butlers…" Henry stopped, realising the significance of the pained expression she could not keep off her face. "Oh, hell. You've met Mother."

Juno sniffed. "She does *not* approve of your choice of bride, if that was a possibility that kept you up at night."

Juno had been dreading this, preparing herself for him to choose his mother over his wife. To declare that after all this whole marriage business between them had been a horrible mistake. Instead, he was as *Henry* as possible. "Well, then," he said with a solemn nod. "We had better hurry up and get this ghost vapour business sorted."

She kissed him again, more thoroughly this time. For once, the passenger was quiet within her, instead of the usual kicking and fretting. Perhaps Juno's comfort in her husband's presence had a soothing effect. "Tell me your news," she said, once his eyes were satisfyingly glazed, and the tension in his frame had finally begun to relax. "What was so important about this little tea party, that you let yourself be dragged out of retirement?"

Serving the Queen, of course, and standing at her side for any social support she required until she found herself a proper husband, was one of those things that went along with being the Duke of Storm. Henry could no more retire from that family tradition than he could from his oft-neglected seat in the Court of Lords. But Juno had the distinct impression when he began packing for this particular trip that it was one of the other missions, the top secret ones from which he was, most certainly, supposed to be retired.

Henry sighed, burying his face in the softest curve of

her neck. "It is the only matter anyone is concerned with, from one end of the Teacup Isles to the other. The choosing of a prince consort."

Juno was surprised at that. "But I thought it was settled. What with the Great Divorce, and…"

It had been the biggest piece of gossip of the social year: Juno should know, as she had spread it to enough people. Only the closest of friends and confidantes, naturally.

Lord Manticore and his former wife Lady Persimmon had recently parted ways and legally ended their marriage: she to marry her mistress, he (so it was generally assumed) to finally put an end to the greatest will-they-won't-they question of Queen Aud's reign.

"Indeed," Henry groaned, the sound vibrating through Juno's collarbone. He got distracted for a moment, tracing her skin with his lips. "The entire court was waiting with bated breath for this wretched love match of theirs to be consummated. But politics reared its ugly head once more… and I have never seen two people more dedicated to mutual suffering for the sake of diplomacy than her majesty and Lord Manticore."

"It's to be a Continental prince consort, then," Juno sighed. Hopefully one who did not mind too much that the Queen he married had already given her heart away to her Advisor on Magical Matters.

"Narrowed down to the royal families of Arunia, Gedos and Trevental," Henry agreed. "Which I would have told you, love, as soon as matters were concluded, and I returned to your side…"

"I know," said Juno, kissing the top of his head, even as he dipped lower, to the neckline of her old black taffeta. "I did not put myself in the middle of your diplomatic night-

mare deliberately, darling. It was an unfortunate conflu-
ence of events."

"And surprise brothers-in-law," Henry muttered.
"Never mind that now. I am glad you're here, Juno. Even if
I'll be out of my head worrying about you the whole time.
I'd much rather have you at my side than anywhere else in
the world." His hands ran lightly over the black fabric. "I
don't suppose you care to remove this dress any time
soon?"

Juno leaned back on the cushions. They had been
provided with a proper bed, at least, instead of some
lopsided hammock. "I couldn't possibly," she said, purring
low in her throat. "That's your job, husband."

~

It was raining when Juno awoke. The rocking of
the ship, so soothing when she first drifted off in
the naked arms of her husband, had shifted tempo just
enough that she found herself staring at the roof of the
stateroom, unable to drop off back to sleep.

The sky, viewed through the brass-rimmed port-holes,
was grey from cloud, and barely light enough to be called
morning. Nevertheless, she dressed swiftly — back in her
rustling mourning blacks, with no alternative readily to
hand — and left Henry sleeping in the bed. Every time she
donned this gown by choice, it felt like more pockets had
been added — some tied on, others sewn into secret seams.
It was funny to think of her old life, where one had to keep
things constantly in little pouches attached to clothing,
because one didn't feel secure even in a private room of
one's own house.

Having conceded the territory of Storm North to the
Dead Dowager Duchess, Juno was in need of pockets

again. One containing a glass bottle waiting for use. Another still stretched wide by the *Shipping Almanac* in case that came in handy again. What her pockets did not contain any longer was a certain hand-written letter from her first husband.

On deck, there were only a handful of sailors around, and they paid Juno little heed. The wide bay around them was full of ships, bright with their banners, clustered in their country groupings.

The Teacup Isles were represented by four ships in all, including the late-arriving *Caliban*. Perhaps the Queen had arranged for the delivery of teacups by privateer in order to have a larger retinue in total. The countries of Arunia, Gedos and Treventral each had only one royal flagship and two support ships.

The *Majestic Harvest*, the ship containing the Queen and her court, was close enough that Juno could see the gleaming sparkle where a magical protective dome had been set around it by magisters overnight.

Their own vessel, the *Bonny Elk*, was likewise protected because of the threat made against Henry by a certain necromantic assassin. That explained why no rain was currently falling to the deck, though the skies continued to pour water down upon the churning seas around them. The good weather had all been used up yesterday; they had to hope the royal breakfast would be held indoors.

Why was Henry the one who had become the target of an assassin? The Queen trusted his advice, it was true, but he hardly had more influence over a choice of royal husband than Lord Manticore, or the Seabournes, or one of the Queen's many elderly great-aunts, all of whom had research dossiers the size of their wardrobes listing the dos and don'ts of every possible suitor from the Continent and beyond.

Juno and Henry would have to put some serious thought into considering who might benefit from his assassination… but not yet. First, Juno had some business to conclude with Vance.

Avoiding the sailors on deck, Juno made directly for the bow, where a graceful sculpture of a mermaid adorned the front of the ship. She had noticed it when she first came aboard: particularly, the small crack between the arch of the mermaid's shoulder blades, and the prow of the ship.

Now, Juno pushed her fingers into that cavity, drawing out the crumpled remains of her first husband's letter. She had not wanted to keep it close at hand, as it would have been impossible to share intimacies with Henry if she imagined even for a second that Vance was watching them unseen. "Come on out then," she said, unfolding the envelope. "Time to talk."

"Have a little respect for the letter," grumbled Vance as he appeared, leaning against the rail. "It's the only thing keeping me here."

"You're lucky I don't throw it overboard," Juno snarled. "You lied to me, Vance. Trying to make me feel sorry for you, so I'd persuade Dominic on your behalf. I'm done with you. Find your own passage to the afterlife."

"Wait, Juno. Please. You don't understand what it's like to be dead," he said, and there it was. The charm, the wide eyes, the authenticity. Somehow Vance had always been able to believe his own balderdash — it was his secret to getting his own way. He never had to scare people like Dominic. He just believed so hard they would do what he wanted… somehow the world shifted to make it happen.

Until, of course, it stopped.

"I don't need to understand," Juno snapped, holding the letter over the water. "I have a new husband. A new life. You're supposed to be gone."

Widowhood might only be a temporary state when one was between marriages, but it was not supposed to be be *revoked*. Vance's widow was not and never again would be his wife.

"You think I don't know that, honey bee? Everything about this existence feels wrong."

She hesitated, the letter still held fast in her hand. Why couldn't she let go? "You heard Dominic. Either you believe he knows nothing, or you don't. If he didn't kill you, that leaves your father as the obvious culprit. Bertram Von Trask might have been a monster, but at least he had the good manners to stay dead."

There was a flash of light across the water. Juno turned, staring out at the bay.

An arrow point, or something like it, amber-bright against the wet grey sky. Then another, like a flame shooting, falling... against the charmed dome that surrounded the *Majestic Harvest*.

"Attack!" cried a sailor from the crow's nest. All in a rush, there were more crew and soldiers and magisters and spellcrackers on the deck than Juno had realised were even aboard.

"When my brother does something, he does it thoroughly," said Vance, his gaze on the royal flagship.

No, that wasn't right. Dominic said he was after Henry, not the Queen... Why would a dangerous magical assassin bother to lie? He had her in his power at the time.

But, of course. By telling her who his target was, he ensured that the Queen and Henry had been separated. Juno felt like she was almost, *almost* within reach of an answer.

"Did the attack breach the dome?" she asked, trying to see.

Her majesty would be fine. She had Lord Manticore

on board with her, and Thornbury Seabourne, and all manner of other magisters and spellcrackers. She had Mneme, most annoying of all, who was *Juno's* dear friend and cousin-in-law, not the Queen's. She could rather do with the emotional support right now, frankly.

"Juno!" Henry crossed the deck, wrapped in his dressing gown.

"We weren't attacked," she assured him. There had been no further magical arrows in the air. "Something shot at the *Harvest*."

Henry stood protectively behind her, one hand resting on her waist. "Her majesty," he said, worried.

"They were the smallest of missiles. I'm not even sure what kind of magic…" Juno blinked. "Oh no."

She saw it now: smoke billowing up off the other ship's deck, rising to fill the magical dome that was still, impossibly, in place. As they watched, the dome shimmered and disappeared, freeing the smoke to plume upwards into the driving rain.

"Fire," Juno breathed. "The flagship is on fire."

13

STORMING THE FLAGSHIP

The next few minutes went by in a terrifying blur. Smoke billowed up out of the royal flagship, crackling with unnatural colours and lights.

Juno saw flames at one point, and caught her breath. Queen Aud was on that ship. Mneme was on that ship.

Henry, of course, threw himself into heroic action, leaping into one of the dinghies sent out from the *Bonny Elk*, closest ship to the *Majestic Harvest*. Before he left, he kissed Juno quickly and said "Stay exactly here," in the firmest of voices.

People were leaping off the burning ship, into the water.

"This is familiar," murmured Vance, her least favourite husband.

"Why do you feel the need to speak," Juno grumbled.

"Seriously," he said, looking paler than usual. "I think I… was there a fire on a ship? Was there magic raining down upon it?"

"What are you talking about?"

"Juno, I died on a *ship*."

She glanced quickly around. Everyone was so busy rescuing or watching the rescue that they were unlikely to pay attention to a duchess talking to thin air. "Hunting accident. They both said that. You went on a hunting trip. By *portal*, because no one ever tried to stop men using portal magic in the history of anything. No ships were involved."

Vance's dark eyes flickered a little, as if his ghostly presence had met with some interference. "What were we hunting?"

"I don't know. Why would I know that? Hunting is almost as despicable as your father's entire sorry business empire. Leave me alone." Juno let the letter fall to the deck of the ship and moved to the side, to get a better view.

She could see the Queen, garbed in a simply enormous dressing gown, bundled into a rowboat with two of her ladies-in-waiting. A new magical dome of preservation set around her in particular.

There was Mneme, coming up out of the water and climbing into a rescue ship steered by none other than Captain Bones. Metis was nowhere in sight — yet again, managing to avoid the attention of her concerned relatives.

"Juno." Vance again, still trying to make this sorry scene all about him. She was so sick of giving him any attention at all.

She could not see Henry. He was out there somewhere, exposed. If anyone — if *Dominic* was going to assassinate him, now would be the time.

"Juno!"

"What?" she snapped, whirling around. "What do you want, Vance?"

She could see the rail of the deck through him. His tidy beard, his poised body language, even his irritating smirk.

All fading from the world. This was not the usual translucence of a spirit. He was leaving.

"I remember how I died," he breathed, the shape of him becoming light and shadow.

Transient vapour.

"No you don't," she yelped, rummaging in the many secret pockets of her widow's gown. "Wait, just a minute."

"I forgive you," Vance said, as his spirit departed.

"Don't you dare," she replied furiously. The very idea, that he had the gall to forgive *her* (for what, she could not possibly imagine) after everything *he* had put her through.

Vance Von Trask faded out, leaving nothing behind but a greyish vapour that hung in the air for a moment.

Juno reached the rail just in time. She released the lid of the bottle, and heard a terrifying, soulful sucking sound as the vapour found its way into the glass.

Her hand shook as she capped the stopper. Finally.

It didn't matter that Vance's revelation came at the least convenient moment (typical of the man!) or that he hadn't had the decency to share his secrets before he passed on. Juno was free of him forever.

Why did she feel like crying?"

"Make way!" cried a voice as more rescue dinghies were released from the side of the *Bonny Elk* into the water. Juno was jolted as two sailors hurried past her. The bottle, slippery in her fingers, fell.

"No," she cried, snatching for it with both hands, and gasping in relief as it settled, cold and solid, between her palms. Safe.

"Look out!" cried another voice and Juno turned just in time to dodge a swinging rope. Something knocked into her from behind and she felt herself sliding, falling…

And then there was only water.

*J*uno saw three ghosts on the day of her second wedding.

Her living cousins, Agate and Amethyst, stayed the night with her at her mother's house in Grey Mare, along with their maids. They wanted to be there in the morning to help her with her dress (gold silk, with an antique ruby pendant gifted to her by the Duke to match the family wedding band he would put on her finger) and tell Bettina what to do with her hair, and so on.

Opal, the dead cousin, drifted alongside them both as always, locked to the charm bracelet on Agate's wrist, which had been Opal's before she died.

It was nice to see them: to listen to their chatter, as she prepared for her new life; and of course, she needed the moral support to deal with her mother, whose social climbing ambitions had been met with such a thorough victory that she did not quite know what to do with herself.

"All worthwhile," Mrs Brooks was often caught muttering into thin air. "Worth the sacrifices. Mother of a duchess!"

Juno had tried to convince her mother to move to the Isle of Storm with her, to take up residence in the Dowager Cottage on the grounds of Storm North. Mrs Brooks refused to leave Grey Mare or the Isle of Thyme. ("What is the point of marrying one's daughter to a duke if one doesn't get to boast about it in the same shops one has patronised all one's life!" was her reply. Referring to herself as 'one' was a new affectation, directly related to the afore-mentioned betrothal of her daughter to a duke.)

Henry and Juno arranged the smallest, fastest possible ceremony that was allowed by good taste and social convention. It was all they wanted after the public disaster of his last 'wedding.'

Her mother was consoled about the lack of general pomp by their choice to be married in Grey Mare, as well as the provision of a golden carriage with four white horses so that the bride and groom could be seen by everyone on their brief journey around the town square.

Her local temple was perhaps not the most auspicious place to be married, but Juno could never explain to anyone why she felt that way. No one else saw the screaming, weeping, bloodstained woman on her knees by the side of the road, garbed in a wedding gown two centuries old: the tale of her tragedy was a popular one in local ballads, but Juno was the only person she knew who could say what colour the bride's hair had been, or comment on the violet embroideries upon her sleeves.

Finally, the ghost of the old priest was standing at the entrance pillars of the temple. He was quicker to greet them than the new priest, who had not quite mastered the time management skills required for his position, and was still busy at the back of the temple, pouring perfumed oils, and lighting candles.

"Nice to see you again, Rheia," the old priest said, calling Juno by her mother's name as he always did.

Juno had mastered the art of politely acknowledging ghosts with a minute smile and tiny nod, without attracting the attention of those around her who did not see them. She did this now; he was the priest who had presided over her naming ceremony, and her mother's, and grandmother's. He deserved a little courtesy.

The wedding ceremony was swift and restrained: only Juno's mother and cousins attended from her side. Mneme and Metis represented the Seabourne-Jupiter side of the family, with no aunts in sight, thank goodness. Mr Thornbury stood up for Henry.

The ring was beautiful: a huge and ancient ruby, matching the pendant around her neck. It felt warm when Henry slid it on to her finger, and Juno saw nothing but the merry gleam in his eyes as they spoke their vows.

Marriage to this man would be fun. She was certain of it.

It was all over very quickly and then they were out in the sunshine again, blinking. Juno was a wife again. She was a duchess, whatever that meant.

Only afterwards, as she was preparing for her wedding night in the beautiful lace-draped bedroom at Storm Bolt on the Isle of Town, did she realise that she had not seen Opal at the side of Agate and Amethyst when the cousins were throwing rice. Nor had she seen the priest again, as they left the temple, or even the wailing ghost-bride in the street.

In fact, for the next fifteen months, she did not see a single ghost.

She was cured.

∽

*T*he water closed over Juno's head, pushing her down. She flailed, trying to swim up, but the layered black taffeta dragged on her limbs, made heavy by the water. Dash it, all those pockets. How could she rise up and save herself when she had a *Shipping Almanac* buried in her dress?

Struggling, she barely managed to lift her head up, out of the water long enough to gasp for air. Sparks burst behind her eyes as she choked on her first clear breath, and cold rain fell around her wet face.

Juno could hear shouting above her, but she didn't know if anyone had even seen her fall. She was further from the ship than she should be, and her body felt so, so heavy.

She could not drown. Not with the passenger aboard. Not…

The water was choppy here. There were boats everywhere, but none close to her. Keeping her head above water was too hard. She was so dratted tired.

Juno sucked in another breath, as the sea sucked her down.

~

Juno was staring into a mirror, though the face looking back at her was not her own: an older woman, graceful and poised, with a vintage silver wig coiled up in formal shape. Her gown was blue, studded with pearls.

She was the Duchess of Storm.

"Antiope," said a familiar voice behind her. Her sister.

(No, Juno had no sister, only cousins.)

"Galatea," she drawled. "Anyone would think you were not pleased to see me. Here. In my own house."

~

The water was dark over Juno's head. She was not even sure which way was up any more. Her gown was so very, very heavy under the water.

With swollen, stiff fingers, she used the last of her energy to untie her pockets, watching them bob away from her into the darkness.

So that was the way up.

"*You can't do this, Antiope,*" Aunt Seabourne — Galatea — *said in the room full of warm, bright things.*

"*This isn't what ghosts do.*"

"*How quickly you forget,*" *said Juno — Antiope — the Duchess of Storm. "I have always been extraordinary. Why would I be any different as a ghost?*"

"*She has her own life,*" *Galatea said sharply. "And yours is done, my dear.*"

"*That's where you're wrong.*" *She could feel her own power, building within her. The house was hers. Entirely hers. Why stop there?*

Antiope had always known exactly who she was, and of what she was capable. She had more spirit than anyone she had ever known.

"*You can't haunt a person, sister,*" *protested Galatea Seabourne.*

The Duchess of Storm smiled dangerously into the mirror.

"*Watch me.*"

14

TORNADO ON A TEA TRAY

*J*uno's eyes snapped open. She stared at the wooden ceiling for a moment, trying to work out if that was her uneasy stomach moving back and forth, or if she was on another ship.

Her lungs hurt. Her limbs hurt.

She sat up too fast, and was caught by a wave of dizziness, and nausea almost as overwhelming as during her first few months sharing her body with the passenger.

Oh no, not again.

"Other side!" cried an alarmed, female voice as Juno lurched to the left.

She caught herself and swung over the other side of the bed, only to find a handy chamberpot waiting for her to throw up into.

"Better?" asked her girl companion, sounding anxious.

"Much," said Juno, which was a lie. She never felt better after casting up her accounts. Every instance felt like a failure.

Early pregnancy had been supremely hard on her sense of personal dignity. She had barely eaten anything for months but lemon-thyme wafers and ginger tea. She came close to wasting away altogether. Even now, Henry looked ever so relieved when he saw her consume something substantial, like an actual slice of bread and butter, or a boiled egg. She had never felt less like a duchess than she had with all that retching and swooning. Thank goodness the passenger had finally taken pity upon her and steered them both into calmer waters.

"I suppose you'd better tell me who you are, and where I am," said Juno finally, recovering a little spirit. Enough to take in her surroundings, at least.

A private cabin of someone important, she guessed, given that she was in an actual bed, the chamberpot she had flung herself at so recently was pure porcelain, and the young lady watching her from the corner was wearing a simply darling tea gown with pink roses all over it. She had long braids and a melancholy air about her.

Pink and gold bunting hung everywhere, with a banner depicting the family coat of arms of the royal family of Trevental (three tulips, a sword made of roses and a field of poppies), so Juno could make an educated guess as to which foreign country was currently hosting her onboard their ship. Still, it would not hurt to be properly introduced to her hosts, and to gain some intelligence.

Such as, what had occurred between her near-drowning experience, and waking up in this sturdy mahogany bed? Had anyone summoned a doctor to check that all was well? When had her current husband last been seen alive?

While she waited for a response to her first demands, Juno peered under the covers and discovered in a numb sort of shock that she was finally free of the dread black taffeta: instead, she wore a voluminous nightshirt in clean white linen, sprigged with peonies, and smelling slightly of camphor wood.

"My name is Laenia," said the girl in the rose dress. "You're on my brother's ship, *Hope-In-The-Mist*."

"And your brother would be…" Juno racked her brain lightly for eligible royals of the Continent. The newspapers had been full of them in recent months, largely because the question of whether or not there was ever to be a royal wedding had risen from a simmer to a bubbling frenzy since the summer. "Prince Sauvon of Trevental," she declared in mild triumph. At least her memory had not been affected from her recent underwater adventure. "Did he rescue me?"

"Actually, that was Duc Rudolf of Gedos," said Princess Laenia. "It was all very dramatic. Our ships were heading across the bay to help with the rescue effort, and then he dove in to save you! Our ship was closer than his by the time he had brought you to the surface, what with all the back and forth. Once he landed on our deck, Comte Georges of Arunia came across in a dinghy to find out what was happening. He likes to be in the middle of things," she added. "That's how he gets into so many scrapes."

Duc Rudolf. Comte Georges. Both popular candidates for the Queen's hand, according to the newspapers, as was their cousin Prince Sauvon. The populace of the Teacup Isles were divided between those who adored Lord Manticore and those who loathed him, which left plenty of people to support the idea of a foreign royal in the Queen's bed.

Honestly, Juno thought at times that the Teacup Isles would be happy with Queen Aud marrying a random footman, as long as they got the chance to purchase a souvenir plate and sigh wistfully over whether or not her royal wedding dress had a train.

All three of the Queen's potential future husbands were here on the same ship. That was interesting. Or it might be, on literally any other day.

Juno pushed back the covers, ready to face the world. "Does anyone know the current whereabouts of my husband, the Duke of Storm? I'd very much like to see him. Immediately."

"Oh," said Laenia, looking sad. "I haven't heard. I'd tell you if I knew. I like to know things. I'll definitely try to overhear something for you!"

The door opened and an extremely handsome (very young) man with bright green hair tied into a tidy queue walked through Laenia's body, as if she was thin air. She sighed and disappeared into a greyish mist.

Of course she was a ghost. She was the first person who had shared useful information with Juno in some time.

"I take it you're Prince Sauvon," Juno said heavily.

The ghost princess did not look to be returning any time soon, so she would have to interrogate the living.

"No, Sauvon's my cousin," said the green-haired prince, taken slightly aback. "I say. Are you the Duchess of Storm? Sauvon swore you were, but my other cousin Rudolf says you're much too young, and you were dressed like a widow when he fished you from the drink. So we don't know what to think. Sorry, I'm Georges. Sorry."

"Is the Queen alive?" Juno asked, since his babbling was beginning to annoy her. He wasn't that much younger than she was, but she found him exhausting.

"Oh, yes. I believe so. Why? What have you heard?" The poor creature was clearly starved for gossip, and/or desperate for someone to tell him what to do. (He had better not win the hand of the queen; she would eat him alive.)

Juno summoned enough strength for a polite smile. "I think I'd better speak to you and your cousins all together, don't you? Assuming you have something appropriate for me to wear."

She would not ask how it was that she, soaking wet, had apparently been stripped and redressed in a dry night-shirt before being tucked into bed. Sometimes you simply did not want to know answers to certain questions.

~

*P*rince Sauvon of Trevental had clearly planned to impress his intended betrothed. His state-rooms included a majestic parlour (probably not called a parlour on a ship, but Juno had lost patience with learning the nautical words for things) adorned with many of the flowers for which his nation was so famous. Peonies, poppies and pimpernels covered every surface: fabrics, engravings, oil paintings and the flowers themselves, covered in preservation spells to stay fresh and pink, pink, pink.

It was like taking tea at a flower market, only margin-ally more elegant.

The prince himself was pretty enough to model for a tailoring magazine. He looked like a watercolour sketch of a person, all pale skin, vivid rose-coloured hair, and a tiny pair of wire-rimmed glasses on the end of his nose. He wore long, scooped tunics in embroidered layers (roses over irises over rhododendrons, every pattern fighting against the others in pink, cream and gold) over tight white stock-ings and pointed boots with a carnation pattern stamped into the leather.

Juno no longer wondered where the nightgown she wore had come from, or indeed the voluminous embroidered dressing garment (covered in ivy, jasmine, forget-me-nots and violets) with which she had been provided by some sort of sea valet.

Again, there was undoubtedly a more appropriate shipboard term for the fellow, but she did not care to learn it.

The other gentlemen in the room were just as finely dressed, but rather less committed to a floral motif.

Georges, the green-haired puppy, wore the national dress of Arunia, which made him look rather like he had escaped a folk dancing competition: far more ribbons than anyone every needed to wear unless the actual goal was to die by random strangulation.

Then there was Duc Rudolf, who appeared to have made his own fashion choices by staring in the mirror and asking himself what his cousins Sauvon and Georges would never be seen dead wearing. He was in black, with touches of red: a swoosh of satin lining, small ruby studs in his ears; he wore his hair long and dark, like a prince out of a fairytale.

Henry approved of this one, Juno recalled. He seemed to think Rudolf had a good head on his shoulders, compared to the rest of them. Best of a bad bunch. Did that mean Henry would have supported Rudolf's suit to the queen?

More importantly, was Henry's partiality for Duc Rudolf of Gedos known widely enough that Juno could rule the man out as a suspect for hiring the Ghost to assassinate her husband? After all, he'd have to be a special kind of fool to arrange the death of a royal courtier who was on his side.

"I suppose I should thank you all for rescuing me," said Juno, employing her own special form of diplomacy.

Laenia had informed her that it was Duc Rudolf who did the actual rescuing, but there was no point in making the other two royal gentleman feel like they had not also been of equally heroic assistance. "What have I missed during my repose?"

~

Quite a lot, as it happened. While Juno was fighting for breath in the water (and fainting like a damsel, which was the part of the story she planned to edit out when relating it to her loved ones) a great rescue had been undertaken of everyone aboard the burning royal flagship.

Queen Aud had been transported to safety, along with the many ladies, magisters, guards and servants aboard the ship. No one had died.

Juno did not ask where her husband or the Queen had been taken, and from the various pieces of news blurted at her by the terribly helpful young Georges, it seemed that none of the royal suitors had any idea.

They were rather more concerned that the royal breakfast had been postponed, with talk of a luncheon now in the wind.

"It's almost like no one wants this little gathering to go ahead," drawled Rudolf with a pointed look at both of his cousins.

Perhaps that was it. General sabotage, rather than a specific grudge against Henry in particular.

A horrible idea crossed Juno's mind, but she rejected it instantly. Lord Manticore was not her favourite person, but he was the type to stand by staunchly, suffering from his passion for the Queen forever, rather than hire someone to stop her doing her duty.

The time for him to do something, or say something, was before this whole wretched tea party was arranged in the first place.

"What exactly are you implying?" snapped Prince Sauvon. "If anyone was going to sabotage the gathering, it was you, Dolf. We all know you're the favourite."

"Says the perfumed prince," sighed Rudolf.

The three of them began squabbling, as a maid (sea maid? ship's matess?) wearing a pink and gold tailored gentleman's suit and beautifully-tied cravat, came around with a tea trolley (sea tea trolley?) laden with: a large teapot, tiny pink cakes that smelled of roses, and thin green crackers that smelled of, well, salt.

"I wouldn't eat any of that," said a solemn voice from the corner.

Juno glanced up discreetly and saw that Laenia the ghost princess had returned. She still wore a floral frock, but the roses all over her dress had gone black, and looked rather sorry for themselves.

Juno had practiced communicating with ghosts in the presence of the living, and rather hoped that her eyebrows spoke for themselves.

"My brother Sauvon put a sleeping draught on the cakes," explained Laenia. "I believe his plan is to knock everyone unconscious so he can return you to your husband and earn favour from the queen. He does that sort of thing, I'm afraid. Mother gave him such a talking to last month for putting sleeping draughts on all his friends in order to win a game of boules."

Juno rolled her eyes. She did not object to a plan that involved reuniting her with Henry, but being drugged seemed an unnecessary complication, especially considering she had the wellbeing of the passenger to think about. No more sleeping potions for her, thank you very much!

Thoughtfully, she tapped a finger in the direction of the green crackers, turning her eyebrows into another question.

"Georges had the same plan," Laenia sighed. "Only he was much less careful with the dosage. Honestly, they are silly."

Well, that was that. Juno would have to dedicate the next year or so of her life to ensuring that neither of these incompetent ninnies got anywhere near her queen.

Thoughtfully, she glanced in the direction of Duc Rudolf, apparently the only gentleman in the room who had not drugged the food. To her surprise, the beautiful long-haired foreign duc was gazing directly at her. Clearly he had noticed her wild eyebrow communication with the empty corner.

As they looked at each other, gazes locked, Juno saw in the periphery of her vision, Prince Sauvon reach out past the rose-pink cakes to take a green cracker, just as Comte Georges reached out past the green crackers to take a rose-pink cake.

Both bit and chewed, thinking themselves safe. Juno did not stop them.

There was something familiar about the calm expression in the eyes of Duc Rudolf, though she could swear she had never met him before.

"That's not my cousin, by the way," murmured Princess Laenia. "Rudolf is more sort of chattery. This one stays still all the time, watching everyone and everything. He's an imposter. I hope you don't mind me telling you things. When I was alive, my friends got terribly annoyed at me for telling their secrets to the maids, and my maids were furious at me telling their secrets to the butlers, but what's the point of secrets if you don't tell them to simply everyone?"

Juno had tuned her out already. Her attention was firmly on the final Continental suitor, whose gaze was locked on to hers. Slowly, she blinked.

Duc Rudolf — not Duc Rudolf, apparently — blinked.

Prince Sauvon and Comte Georges both slumped unconscious to the floor.

No one flinched.

"Where's your ring, Dominic?" Juno asked in a heavy voice. The hands of 'Duc Rudolf' were bare. No silver skulls in sight. But as soon as she asked herself the questions "who would bother to impersonate one of the Queen's suitors?" and "where have I seen that body language before?" she knew exactly who she was looking at.

The false Duc Rudolf blew out a breath. "By gods," he said in frustration. "Can I *hire* you?"

"You couldn't afford me," said Juno, with some satisfaction.

15

DRESS FOR THE WEATHER
YOU WANT

Gingerly, Juno stepped around the unconscious bodies of the diplomats (such as they were). "I'm starting to suspect — and correct me if I'm wrong — that you're not actually planning to assassinate my husband."

Dominic sighed. "What makes you think that?"

"To be honest, I think you'd be better at it than this." Juno glanced behind her, to the corner where the dead girl stood, her entire gown wilting dark: roses and fabric and all. "We're leaving," she informed her. "Want to come?"

Princess Laenia shook her head. "I stay on the ship," she said softly. "Forever. I'm tethered here. I don't mind, though. Ever so many interesting things happen on this ship. It was nice able to tell someone all about them, for once."

"Good travels to you, then," said Juno, trying not to feel sad for the girl. "Thank you for your help."

"Where is it you think we're going?" Dominic asked as they left the cabin together. "I need to be here."

"Well, I need to be at Henry's side," said Juno, leading

the way to the other cabin, the fancy stateroom where she had woken up. "And I think you know exactly where he is."

"I still have information to glean from those two sleeping pratfalls," Dominic hissed in an undertone.

Juno rolled her eyes at him. She had been doing that a lot lately. "What could they possibly know would be of use to you?"

He had no answer.

At the doorway to the cabin, she turned slowly. Now she was used to seeing the workings of Dominic on the handsome stranger's face, she was certain she could read him rather well. "Will it be professionally embarrassing for you if I guess?"

"I need to know which of them hired the Ghost to kill the Duke of Storm," Dominic said fiercely. "Did your ghost offer any useful intelligence?"

"You're *the* Ghost. Don't you know who hired you?"

"Not always," he grated.

"If you're not going through with it, why does it matter?" But, of course. Of course, it mattered. Juno let out a short laugh. "Oh, I *see*."

"You don't see anything."

"I know a Queen's man when I see one."

Surrounded. Juno was perfectly surrounded by the fellows. Did Will know about Dominic? Did Dominic know about Will? Had they been working together, all along? Or were they both blundering around in the dark?

Dominic's eyes flared. He opened the stateroom door in a hurry and pushed Juno through. When the door was closed behind them, he dropped the illusion charm. Duc Rudolf's hair and face fell away, to be replaced by cheek-bones carved out of stone, and an icy glare to match. "You know nothing," he snarled.

126

"Believe me," said Juno. "On this particular subject, I am a world expert."

She swanned across the stateroom to examine her black taffeta silk, now a rather sad specimen hanging from a hook. The gown was salt-crusted and still too damp to think about wearing, even if she wanted to.

She would need something more suitable than a dressing gown, but this was not it.

"How did you know?" Dominic asked from the doorway.

Juno began to rifle through the black gown's folds, locating and detaching the various pockets she needed. She had released several of them, when she was drowning. It looked like the *Ship's Almanac* was gone forever. The vial containing Vance's spirit essence was still there, along with her money purse and a few other necessities.

She shifted everything important to one of her more portable pockets, and untied it neatly from the hidden loop beneath a bunch of damp taffeta. Then, and only then, did she answer Dominic's question.

"Because I am observant. Don't worry, your secret is safe, if you're so bothered."

"Bothered? My life and reputation depends on that secret staying safe."

"Well, then. It's a good thing I'm so trustworthy. And that I'm the only person on this ship who can apparently communicate with its very gossipy ghost."

Juno whisked herself over to the prince's wardrobe and started to sort through it. Continental fashions for men were rather looser fitting than gentlemen's clothes in the Teacup Isles, which suited her purposes nicely. She would be able to fit into Prince Sauvon's breeches (there was a pair covered in carnations that rather caught her eye) and soft linen shirts, which were designed to be worn beneath a generous waistcoat and layered, floating jacket.

Perhaps not the waistcoat, she decided, though there was one covered in cornflowers that she rather coveted. Generous the cut may be, but the tailor did not have the hips of a lady in mind when he cut the cloth, nor the belly curve of a future heir in progress.

She swept past a violet coat, and an emerald one, to find a gloriously red flared silk coat with silhouettes of roses and thorns embroidered over the sleeves.

"You plan to be highly visible from afar, then?" remarked Dominic.

"Shh," said Juno. "It has buttons all the way to the neck, which is what I need right now in a coat. Turn around, please, so I may dress myself."

What she wouldn't give to have her maid along on her adventure. *Oh, Bettina. I will never abandon you again.*

~

*I*t took Juno some time to clothe herself — it was a while since she had clambered into men's breeches, and it was not a knack she had ever especially mastered.

Dominic was quiet for the most part, which made her highly self-conscious of all her rustlings, huffings and strainings. Still, it could be worse. Given how much interest the former Duchess of Storm had taken in her sartorial choices, Juno was lucky she had not ended up fumbling with a waterlogged corset.

That sparked a rather odd memory, of something she had seen, or heard, when she was in the water. Had she dreamed of her mother-in-law?

"Do you still have Vance's letter?" Dominic asked.

"I lost it on the other ship," said Juno. Oh dear. Tact was required, and she wasn't sure she had much of that left. "I no longer need it. I'm afraid — or rather, I suppose we should be pleased — your brother found his satisfaction."

"*What*."

"Don't turn around!" Juno yelped. "Still buttoning."

"I won't. But — are you sure?"

"I captured the transient vapour when he moved on. Found the answer to his question. Whatever the official phrasing is. I'm certain, Dominic."

Finally, she was done with all the tiny buttons. The jacket covered her chest more substantially than was common with gentleman's jacket fashions of the Teacup Isles. It flared almost to her knees, so she could almost convince herself she was wearing a gown. There were remarkably deep pockets, so she didn't have to tie the one from the black taffeta gown to her, merely shoved it deep inside a cavity lined with floral satin.

"I'm nearly ready. Just boots to go. You can turn around."

Dominic looked pale. He always looked pale. But the news of Vance had clearly shaken him. "So, he knew? He told you at the end. He worked out how he died?"

"He did," said Juno. It wasn't a lie. A misdirection, perhaps, but that was what Dominic got for asking more than one question at once.

"You *know*?"

"It doesn't matter," she said firmly. "Dominic. We don't have time for this. You have your own mission. I want to be reunited with my husband."

"My mission is to find out who wants your husband dead," he snapped back.

She rolled her eyes. "If you say so. Laenia, can you join us for a moment?"

The door shimmered, and the ghost girl in her floral frock appeared: now mostly grey and black. "I thought you were leaving," she said curiously.

"We have to leave, indeed. Very soon. But before we go — Laenia, do you know whether your brother or cousins might have wanted the Duke of Storm dead?"

The girl blinked a few times.

Dominic, tense with frustration, followed Juno's line of sight, though he could see nothing.

"Georges doesn't like your husband very much," Laenia said finally. "He's the one most keen to marry your Queen. His inheritance will be capped on his birthday if he can't make this happen and *oh*, he threw such a tantrum when Auntie told him, she shut him up in his bedroom for three days. Sauvon isn't as keen — he only went through with all this to please our family, but he hates the idea of marrying a lady who outranks him. And Rudolf is in love with the Count of Numillia. The Count threw him over, of course, but everyone knows he's wild to win him back once this—"

Juno raised a hand to stem the flow of juicy gossip. Under other circumstances she'd have been glad to pull up a chair and listen to every detail. "Do you think Georges might go to the lengths of hiring an assassin?"

"Oh," said Laenia, looking almost cheerful. "Certainly not, he wouldn't know how. But my stepfather would. Boris Lerange. He's hired assassins at least three times this year. The local guild won't even take his money any more, because he keeps changing his mind and demanding refunds. And I heard him arguing with Sauvon before the boat left — he told him not to worry about the Duke of Storm getting in the way of his plans to take over the Teacup Isles, and Sauvon told him, uh. Where to stick it?"

Juno nodded. "That's extremely helpful, Laenia." A horrible thought crossed her mind. "Is it ill-mannered to ask how you died?"

"I can't really remember," said Laenia. "But it happened here, on the *Hope-In-The-Mist*. We were having a party to celebrate the betrothal between Boris and my mother. I was standing on the starboard deck, and I told him I was going to tell mother what I overheard in the roserie earlier that day, about his mistress and the lapdog, and…" Her eyes widened. "*Oh*."

Juno winced. "No assassins that time?"

"He just pushed me in!" Laenia said indignantly. "Into the water!"

Juno waited, half expecting the girl ghost to disappear in a puff of transient vapour. "Do you feel different?" she asked finally. "Like you want to move on, or…"

"Oh no," said Laenia fiercely. "Boris loves this ship. He holds so many parties here, even though he knows it annoys Sauvon. When we get back to Trevental, I'm going to haunt him *so hard* he'll wish he never messed with me." She blew Juno a kiss, and threw a small handful of rose petals at her, which disappeared into the air one by one. "Thank you! This was very helpful. Safe travels!"

She walked through the nearest wall, with great purpose. The roses on her gown were looking decidedly pink again as she made her exit.

Juno found Dominic gazing at her expectantly. "Well?" he asked.

"The Queen of Trevental's husband," said Juno. "Some fellow named Boris? It sounds like he thought Henry stood in the way of Prince Sauvon's suit."

"Boris Lerange," Dominic growled. "Wonderful. With

131

the size of their treasury he could have hired a dozen magical assassins."

"So it would be a good idea to reach Henry sooner rather than later? Since your job is apparently to protect him, not kill him?"

"I've sorted his protection," Dominic said gruffly. "But don't worry, I'll take you to him. He was an idiot to let you out of his sight."

"Thank you, I think." Juno frowned at him. "What form of transportation did you have in mind?"

Dominic sighed. "We can travel by portal. Speed will be crucial."

"Oh, thank goodness!" she burst out. "Honestly, if I have to set foot in one more boat, I think I will scream."

16

SAILING INTO THE STORM

The pink-jewelled portal in the staterooms of the Prince of Trevental transported Juno and Dominic directly into the middle of nowhere: a scrubby piece of land somewhere on Ghost Island.

Juno frowned at the portal, and then at Dominic, and then at the nearby river. She had a bad feeling about this. She was proved correct when Dominic removed a concealment charm from a small swan-shaped boat currently moored on the river bank.

"Please tell me you're joking," Juno sighed. She could not even muster up a fraction of her usual duchess spirit to inform him she would rather die than set foot in one of those contraptions ever again.

No, she was going to have to be a good sport about this, wasn't she? After all, she had sabotaged Dominic's mission already. He was doing her a favour by escorting her to wherever Henry, the Queen and Juno's friends were holed up.

Still, she seethed with inner resentment. Now that ladies were allowed — even duchesses! — to travel by portal, she had hoped to see the end of boats in general, and swan-shaped boats in particular. But no, this was apparently a week for *all the boats*.

~

The swan-shaped boat was traditionally reserved for the transportation of aristocratic ladies, though it extended to women of the middle classes, and maidservants. Its origins were lost in the mists of time, though Juno had her own theories about the history of boatbuilders, sailing charms, and someone's singular sense of humour.

The *cygneture* enchantment: an ancient and baffling piece of magic, could be laid upon any seaworthy vessel, transforming it into a ruffled, feathered and distressingly anthropomorphised creature halfway between living and something else.

Since the rise of portal magic (exclusively the terrain of gentlemen over the last few centuries), the swan-shaped boat in all its forms — small squashed, medium damp, and large but over-filled — had become synonymous with the transportation of ladies from isle to isle.

Why anyone thought that ladies and their luggage were better subjected to the scent of wet feathers than to a momentary inner heat and pleasant fluttering of the skin caused by a convenient portal was quite beyond Juno. She had thrown all her support behind her friend Mneme Seabourne's recent campaign for equality in magical transportation.

And yet, and yet. Here she was, on a possibly haunted island, stepping into a swan-shaped boat alongside her highly dangerous former brother-in-law.

Life was infuriating at times.

~

"Security," Dominic said shortly, when Juno questioned why the portal had not taken them directly to her husband's location. "Storm's life is still in danger, remember? Not to mention the Queen."

"Perhaps if you had a better system for identifying the people who tried to hire the Ghost, we wouldn't be in this mess," Juno said tartly, arranging her entire lack of skirts on the bench as the swan-shaped boat raised its long, curved neck and began to slowly flap its wings.

The boat moved against the current, propelled upriver by magic and damp feathers. Juno resigned herself to a long and uncomfortable journey.

Still, where there was a long journey, there was the potential for informative conversations. Something to look forward to!

She treated herself to a few minutes of awkward silence, to warm Dominic up before she pounced.

"Why did you never tell Vance the truth about how he died?" she asked, after those minutes had passed.

"I did," Dominic replied. "Many times, when he first began haunting my watch. The first time, he vanished straight after. I thought it was done. But he returned, over and over. He never remembered what I had told him."

"Oh," said Juno, finally understanding. "That's quite common, you know. Ghosts find it difficult to retain new information. They can't change, or grow. They only exist out of their own memories, and if that memory is broken or damaged… well. They get stuck."

"So it wasn't anything you told him," Dominic said, watching her intently. "He figured it out for himself."

Juno gave him a mysterious smile. "He was triggered by being on a ship. Something about being on the *Bonny*

Elk unlocked his memory." But no, it wasn't quite that. It was the magical attack on the *Majestic Harvest* that set him off. Wasn't it?

"That makes sense," said Dominic, looking somewhat ill. That, of course, could be the wet feather smell.

Juno waited. Surely, if she was patient and let him think that she knew all his family secrets, Dominic would let *something* slip.

Not that she needed to know. Of course not. She had merely been dragged from pillar to post in service of a family mystery that had literally haunted her from beyond the grave.

She could wait a little longer.

Dominic's eyes narrowed. "You don't know what he figured out, do you?"

Juno batted her eyelashes. "I'm starting to suspect," she said. "That you don't know either."

He laughed. "And that's it? I just spill my guts to you?"

"Fine, *don't* tell me. How about you tell me something about my current husband. How do I know this isn't all some ruse to use me against Henry? You could be taking me hostage."

"I'm not taking you hostage, Juno," Dominic groaned. "I wouldn't dare."

Perhaps it would take him getting really fed up with her to let down his guard. She was going to have to go full duchess. Juno arched her back, lifted her chin and made an imperious gesture around at the swan-shaped boat. "How exactly would this look different if you *were* taking me hostage?"

"You've made a lot of assumptions about me today," Dominic replied. "If any of them were correct, you must know that I don't have clearance to tell you anything about your husband."

She smiled bitingly back at him. "And you must know that as the Duchess of Storm, I already know all of my husband's secrets."

"Not mine, though," said Dominic Von Trask.

And then, outrageously, he remained silent for the rest of the journey.

~

*V*ance was still on Dominic's mind. Juno was certain of it. When the swan-shaped boat reached its destination, and Dominic rose to hand Juno safely on to the bank, he asked rather abruptly: "Why do you think some people become ghosts, and others do not?"

Juno waited until her feet were safely on the ground before she said: "No one really knows. I spent my younger years consuming every book of lore, philosophy and theories about the spirit world that I could get my hands on. Many people die with some kind of unfinished business outstanding, or from a surprising act of violence. Only a handful of those become ghosts — and only a handful of *those* become the kind of ghosts that can communicate, and hold on to their identity as strongly as Vance did."

Dominic gave her a wry look as he leaped on to the bank beside her. "Honestly, I wouldn't have picked him to have that much strength of personality."

"People can surprise you," she said calmly. They began to walk together along a recently trodden path. She briefly distracted herself by wondering which of the boot patterns belonged to Henry. "It's a bit like being a duke, or a duchess."

"It is?" Dominic seemed amused by her now. All the better to underestimate her.

"Oh, yes," she insisted. "It's all about belief. Confidence. Spirit, you might say. Ghosts are a cluster of memories tethered by some kind of powerful emotion. Love. Rage. Fear."

"Arrogance?"

Juno smirked at him. "What makes you say that?"

Dominic shrugged. "Isn't it the height of arrogance to take up space in the world after you're supposed to have departed? Holding on past the point of no return?"

"Interesting observation," noted Juno. "From a man who chose Ghost as his assassin name."

"I didn't choose that," he said, frowning. "I inherited it."

Juno's eyebrows almost flung themselves off her face. "Oh, I *see*."

"I doubt that you do."

"Spirit is the most appropriate word," she continued. "It has the double meaning. Personal energy. A deep footprint in the world. But yes, arrogance works too."

"And that's what it's like," he said. "To be a duchess."

"Some days, yes. Titles have power. It takes a certain kind of spirit to live up to them."

She had a sudden vivid vision: Antiope Seabourne filling Juno's house, commanding her servants, forcing her into that black taffeta nightmare of a dress. Now there was a woman with spirit.

"And your Duke of Storm, he has all that?" Dominic asked.

"Oh, Henry," Juno said with a sigh. "He doesn't even have to try. He was born into it. He walks through the world with all the confidence of a man whose ancestors built everything he owns."

They came over the rise of the hill. It was beginning to drizzle, because of course they couldn't get through a day without some kind of rain imposing itself on the scene.

Juno's heart lifted as she caught sight of Henry, his familiar silhouette still a good distance away. Wide shoulders, good-humoured face, a well-tied cravat that suggested his valet had seen him more recently than his wife. It felt like days since she had last seen him.

There was Queen Aud, too, sitting beneath a rain parasol near a clifftop, in quiet conversation with a handsome dark-haired fellow who must be the real Duc Rudolf. Henry stood a short distance from them both, close enough to hear everything that was said between them.

Mneme Seabourne and her husband Thornbury were nearer, huddling over a private conversation of their own. Mneme's face lit up as she turned her head and caught sight of her friend.

"*Juno!*" Mneme cried, hurtling in her direction for a hug that started out fierce, then became more careful as she remembered the extra person aboard. "Oh, my dear. We've been so worried. Are you all right — both of you?"

"The passenger is ship-shape, as far as I can tell," said Juno, returning the hug with warm relief. She felt like she had not been properly able to relax since she first saw her dearest people under attack, while she was too far away to help them.

Out of the corner of her eye, she saw Dominic and Thornbury exchange exactly the kind of discreet, wary nod you might expect of two men who had worked in parallel for a long time, under covert circumstances.

Bloody Queen's men. She was sick of the lot of them.

"I'm not just asking about the baby, Juno," scoffed Mneme. "You've had such a time of it. And you were supposed to be at home with your feet up!"

"Believe me," said Juno. "You'd evacuate a house pretty quickly, if your Aunt Antiope had taken up residence."

"That's fair," considered Mneme with a nod. "I used to hide under the stairs from her when I was little." She glanced around. "But where is Henry? I expected him to be with you."

"Don't be silly," said Juno. A cold sort of feeling crept over her. "He's right over there, near the Queen. He's been with you this whole time."

Mneme tilted her head in the direction of the Queen and her suitor, looking puzzled. "Are you sure? I haven't seen him since before our ship was attacked."

Juno felt the passenger lurch within her; a fine time to be kicking and making a fuss. "Mneme," she said steadily. "That isn't my idea of a joke."

"Juno," said Dominic, nearby. "I mean — your grace, damn it. I have something to tell you. Don't—"

Juno could see Henry quite clearly, not far from them all. He had not glanced up to acknowledge her arrival, his gaze fixed intently on the Queen and her suitor. Now that Juno looked more closely, she could see that the drizzle — now becoming heavier — was falling directly through her husband as if he were entirely insubstantial.

"Oh, gods," she said, feeling her stomach lurch with horror. Blackness closed in around her vision, swamping her. "He's a *ghost*."

17

IT'S RAINING GHOSTS

J uno dreamed of Antiope, Duchess of Storm. The ghost
of her dead mother-in-law loomed over her. The red
and white stripes of her gown blazed like the sun.
"You will never be good enough," declared the real Duchess.
"Who do you think you are?"

$\sim$

J t was worth the almost-three hour carriage ride
across the length and breadth of the Isle of
Thyme. Juno and Henry were to spend their wedding night
at a beautiful cliff-side hotel, so exclusively reserved for the
highest of society that Juno had never heard its name
before.

Seventeen different people had called her 'your grace'
since luncheon, and Juno was still not sure how she felt
about the whole thing.

Graceful, after three hours in a carriage, was asking
rather a lot.

They dined on grilled sardines, quail in peaches and a

tower of moulded asparagus. This was followed by elder-flower mousseline, and meringues so delicate you could balance them on a tine of a fork.

Then bed, and all the awkward pleasures of undressing each other for the first time. Everything that followed. Kisses, both hurried and slow. Heat. Laughter.

Juno was delighted to discover that yes, there would be laughter in this marriage. That boded well for the future.

⁓

It was only the next morning, as they lazed about in bed with a breakfast tray, that Juno thought to ask the question.

"What makes you think I can be a duchess? A proper one."

"I prefer improper ones," said Henry, and bit her shoulder a little. Which, at the very least, justified her choice of nightgown: daringly cut with almost no sleeves.

She had no objection to the biting, nor the nuzzling at her breasts, nor the slow, searching kisses that followed. Before long, the breakfast tray and the nightgown had both hit the floor again, and Juno was beneath her husband, gasping into his skin as he… *oh*.

Yes, this was what it was supposed to be like.

⁓

Some time later, when they had reassembled what could be salvaged of the breakfast tray, and Juno had her nightgown back on (if inside out), she returned to her topic. "I'm serious. Is there a handbook? How am I supposed to walk and speak and behave? Will the other duchesses hate me?"

She felt a little queasy at the thought of it. How did one learn to be a duchess? Must she befriend the most highly regarded lady of the same rank, and steal her maid?

"Just walk about in pretty dresses, and the rest will take care of itself," said Henry, snaffling the last of the breakfast rolls.

Juno scoffed at her new husband. "That has to be the most unhelpful advice I've ever heard. Who else do I speak to about this?"

~

"Antiope, leave her alone," begged Aunt Seabourne. "You've done enough. You shouldn't be here."

"And yet," said the Duchess of Storm — the old Duchess of Storm, the always Duchess of Storm. "You can't make me leave, can you, Galatea? All the might of the Royal Society of Mediums, and countless priests at your disposal, and you can't dislodge me."

"Ugh!" cried Aunt Seabourne, throwing up her arms. "You're impossible as always. Wait until your son gets home."

~

For the first (delightful, passionate, amusing) few months of her marriage, Juno avoided Storm North, the family country seat, as much as she possibly could. Town was so bracing, after all! It was true that many of the older ladies among the nobility disapproved of her so heartily that she was going to have to give up her dream of having any kind of duchess mentor, but still. She had actual friends, and that was even better.

She had a husband whose eyes grew warm when he saw her, who teased her and spoiled and lavished his attention on her. A husband, it turned out, who was sometimes a distressingly heroic secret agent of the Crown. But no one was perfect.

"I'm giving it up," he told her one day, as they emerged from a most enlightening encounter on a sofa, which had begun with a little light teasing banter about whether or not it was time for Juno to stop wearing a contraception charm, and ended with Henry buck naked and flat on his back.

Being swept off one's feet by passion was lovely, but oh, Juno also very much enjoyed doing the sweeping.

On this particular occasion, she had barely caught her breath from their sofa romp, and here he was making promises about retirement, determined that the more dangerous side of royal business should no longer be his concern.

He wanted to be there for his family. Juno wanted that with him.

The contraception charm went out the window.

As, later that evening, did another of her nightgowns. Honestly, she might as well stop wearing the dratted things.

~

*A*n impossible, wonderful thing happened. Mneme's campaign to end the social prohibition of portal-travel for ladies (aided by Juno herself, among other useful friends) was finally successful! Popping back and forth between the various ducal houses was no longer a matter requiring luggage and feathers and shipping times and enchanted vessels.

This left Juno with little excuse. Coaxed by Henry, she did indeed begin to spend more time at Storm North, walking the gardens and peering at the wallpaper. She began renovations. Hired more staff.

Unlike the town house, Storm North had both a master and mistress suite of rooms, which meant two completely new beds for them both to enjoy, once Juno had picked out new furnishings for them both. Not to mention the adjoining passage between the suites, which was private but felt ever so scandalous for the occasional daring assignation.

By the time spring turned to summer, and the passenger came aboard, Storm North felt entirely theirs.

More importantly, Juno believed she actually *was* the Duchess of Storm, not merely a new wife playacting the role. Her spirit finally matched the outward airy confidence she had projected from the start.

She was good enough.

She was enough.

She would be mother of the future heir, once she could conquer the complete betrayal of her body that set her both retching and swooning on a regular basis.

She survived that.

She could survive anything.

As long as she had Henry — husband, partner, duke — by her side, then Juno, Duchess of Storm, could master any challenge.

~

"We'll see," said Antiope, Duchess of Storm, ghost in residence. "Won't we?"

Aunt Seabourne huffed in frustration. "And what exactly, my dear, do you mean by that?"

~

*H*enry was dead. Oh, gods. Henry was dead.
Juno had never felt so alone in her life.
The shock of it felt like the loss of her father all over again.
Worse. It felt like the ground had dissolved under her feet.

Henry was a *ghost*.

Was this her future? To be followed around by dead husbands until they attained enough character growth to turn into vapour that could be trapped in a bottle?

Henry was dead.

Widow.

Widow.

Widow.

~

*J*uno opened her eyes. The first thing she saw was a bright blaze of violet and lemon billowing above her. Dark spots flared against the striped silk in a repeating pattern that only made sense when she realised she was lying in a tent, staring at the fabric ceiling. It was raining outside.

"Is this the Queen's tent?" she asked aloud.

"She's worried about you," said an apologetic voice she instantly recognised as that of her (living, breathing, *what?*) husband. "We all are. How do you feel, love?"

"Confused." Juno sat up and stared down at herself. Gone were the elegant floral breeches and high-buttoned jacket she had briefly borrowed from an unconscious prince. She was wearing the black taffeta all over again. Dry as a bone, rustling crisply against the soft sheets. Full of pockets. "Dash it to the Underworld!" she yelled in exasperation. "This bloody *dress*."

"Now," said Henry, in a very careful voice that

146

suggested she was going to get even angrier, very soon. "This is all quite simple to explain, love."

Juno stared wildly at him. He looked like Henry. Perfectly normal. Dressed in his valet's favourite cravat (the one she hated) because of course Mr Marlborough would make the most of this little adventure to take the upper hand.

Served Henry right for leaving his wife at home. He was going to be stuck as a ghost in a less than satisfactory cravat forever.

Except, she was missing something. An important detail.

Henry was perched on the bed, close enough to touch. No translucence. No sign of being anything other than warm and pink and alive.

Slowly, Juno reached out and stuck her finger hard in the middle of his chest.

"Ow," Henry said mildly.

Her eyes narrowed. This time, when she reached out to check he was alive and human and most definitely not dead, it was to shove him very roughly with both her hands. "You're not *dead*."

"Not in the least!" he assured her.

She wanted to smack him. She wanted to shake him until his teeth rattled. "I thought you were a ghost."

"That's my fault," spoke up another voice.

Juno glanced up around and saw Dominic, still wearing the dark formalwear from his guise as Duc Rudolf, standing near the soft wall of the tent with his arms folded. Beside him, warily standing guard: Mr Thornbury Seabourne. Mneme was here too. As soon as Juno's gaze fell upon her, she burst forward to the bed, speaking all in a rush.

"Are you all right? Do you need tea? I can send all

these horrid gentlemen away if you want. Anything you need. Oh, *Juno*."

"You're sweet, Mneme," said Juno steadily. "But what I need is an explanation, so we'll have to suffer these horrid gentlemen a few minutes longer." She locked eyes with Dominic, burning with so much quiet fury that she could not believe she had ever been afraid of him. "Why was my husband a ghost?"

Her former brother-in-law held his hand up solemnly, showing that the skull seal she remembered from his father's hand was back where it belonged. The magic of it mixed and shimmered with his own, giving him a general haze of power.

"Storm here was gracious enough to accept my protection," he began. "While I investigated the matter of the Continental suitors. My family ring uses something like portal magic to mimic the qualities of a ghost: including the option of a diffuse body state. It was the best way I could be sure of not losing your husband to a crossbow bolt the second my back was turned."

"He has other protections," Thornbury said calmly.

"Does he," Dominic replied, equally calm.

"That's how you performed all your little assassinations," said Juno. The Ghost. Of course. Disappeared from locked rooms as if he was never there. A piece of trickery attached to an enchanted ring.

Everyone looked uncomfortable.

She rolled her eyes. "Yes, I get it. Another cover story. You're not an assassin at all, then? Or do we call it something different when you're working for the Crown?"

"It's a long story," said Dominic.

Juno glared harder at him. "I have time. Wait right there until I've finished being furious with my husband. You're next."

"I say!" said Henry, sounding dismayed. "Never mind all that. You need to stay calm, Juno. All this jumping about and nearly drowning and fainting all over the place can't be good for the... uh..."

The word 'baby' was off limits to them both. Henry had suggested that himself, when he first realised how intimidated Juno was at the idea of carrying a child who was a ducal heir, whom everyone would think of as belonging to the hereditary dukedom of Storm, not just their family.

"It's not doing me a power of good either," she said, allowing all her inner grumpiness to show on her face. No more holding back. "Mneme, who put me in this dress?"

"No one," her friend said, frowning. "You weren't wearing it before you fainted. You were in that whole — trouser situation. Very modern. The dress appeared after Dominic picked you up off the ground."

Juno nodded grimly. "Thought so. It's your mother again, Henry. I am being haunted by the one person who thinks *she* is more deserving of my title, my home and my husband."

"Oh," Henry said, looking almost relieved. "Don't worry about that, dearest. Mneme and Thornbury filled me in on the duchess spirit palaver. I've set the right person on the job. Hopefully, the house will be all fresh and ghost free by the time we get home."

Juno frowned at him. She was beginning to feel a headache coming on. "I hope you don't mean Mrs Hawthorn and her medium friends, because she was quite at sea about the whole business when I saw her last."

"Certainly not," said Henry. "I can do better than that!"

"It's my mother," said Mneme. "Don't worry, Juno. If anyone can quell Aunt Antiope, it's..."

～

*G*alatea leaped back as bars appeared over the window. She ran for the door, but it slammed in her face. *"Stop this nonsense, Antiope! You're acting like some kind of monster."*

The face of the Duchess appeared for the moment in the surface of the door, as if it were mirrored glass. "I am as I always was, Galatea. You know me better than most."

～

*J*uno blinked hard. "I think," she said, and then pressed her hands over her mouth as her stomach lurched. Drat the passenger. When would her body feel like her own again? "I think your mother is in very great danger, Mneme."

"Darling, you need to rest," Henry assured her, taking her hand. "We'll sort all this out, but you mustn't take on any more strain."

"Don't think we're done with all your explanations," Juno said sternly. "And apologies, and…" Their hands fell through each other. "Oh," she said weakly. "You're a ghost again."

But no: it wasn't Henry's pinkish hand that was translucent. It was her own. Juno stared at her hands as they faded before her eyes. "That feels odd," she said dimly. "Ever so…"

"Juno," said Dominic, kneeling by her side. He pushed his ring at her, the spiral of skulls catching the light. "Put this on. We can…"

"Oh, I think it's too late for that," said Juno. She gave him a weak smile.

"Juno!" screamed Mneme. Her voice was already too soft, too pale, fading out. Juno was barely there at all…

There was nothing quite so strange as the feeling of disappearing, a little at first and then all at once.

All she knew, as she faded out of that bright striped tent, was that the wretched black taffeta dress was still with her.

Pockets and all.

18

STEALING HER THUNDER

*I*t had been rather a trying few days for Mrs Emmeline Hawthorn: housekeeper to Storm North, long-time family retainer of the Jupiter family and qualified medium (second class).

The house, under the control of the old Duchess, had gone to wrack and ruin. Mrs Hawthorn's attempt to seal the house with enchantments, a standard ritual when the family were 'from home' and the servants given time off, had gone entirely awry.

The ghost of the late Duchess had actually bellowed in her face using a violent illusion formed of chimney smoke, which was not how a good housekeeper ought to be treated.

Only Mrs Seabourne (Mrs Galatea Seabourne, that was, her grace's sister and known longtime family member) had been allowed to darken the door of Storm North, after the chimney smoke incident. She emerged once, to give Mrs Hawthorn some quiet instructions, and then was entirely swallowed up by the house, which was determined to keep anyone else out. Ivy grew instantly over the doors and windows. Bars stretched up and over every window.

A moat appeared, filled with the most distressing creatures.

There had been a moat once before, but that was generations before even her ladyship had been born, when Emmeline was a girl whose mother worked in the big house, so where had it come from now? Goodness only knew.

To top it all off, several self-important ladies from the Royal Society of Mediums had turned up to 'sort the matter out,' taking over the parlour at the Hare and Wicket like bees establishing a new hive.

Mrs Hawthorn, only a second class medium in the society, found herself utterly ignored for the first time in decades. It was most insulting. She ran a household. Not just any household. She was the housekeeper for Storm North, the country seat and oldest family residence of the Duke of Storm. When she spoke, there were usually at least three maids ready to jump to attention or burst into tears.

This would not do.

"I really do not think a seance is advised," she protested as Lady Dorrit, Mrs Smee and Alderwoman Grenfell arranged their cloths and crystals on the parlour table. "This is far from an ordinary haunting."

"With all due respect, Mrs Hawthorn," said Alderwoman Grenfell, not even pausing to make eye contact with her. "We know what we are doing."

Mrs Hawthorn wanted to scream at them all. The old Duchess — Dowager, she should say, though it set her teeth on edge to have the usual rules of addressing the family set aside because people went about returning from the dead — was at least a class six spirit by now, possibly close to a class nine. The Duchess's confident presence and sense of self, not to mention her sheer sense of entitlement to the entirety of Storm North, made her one of the most dangerous spirits that the Royal Society had ever faced.

They were not prepared. They would not listen. They only allowed her at the table because they needed a fourth to make a proper circle — and she had gone along with it after all her protests went unheard because at least if she was here, she might have half a chance of preventing a catastrophe.

Once they realised they were out of their depth, they would, finally, surely, listen to what she had to say.

There was another problem with the Royal Society's plan to summon the old Duchess out of her house, but Mrs Hawthorn didn't realise that until it was too late.

The candles were lit, the crystals were glowing, the hands were held in a circle. The ladies hummed.

"We summon thee from thine haunting," said Lady Dorrit in a deep, dramatic voice. "Come to us and speak, spirit. We name thee and bind thee: Duchess of Storm."

"Wait," Mrs Hawthorn broke in. "Which Duchess of Storm do you mean? *There are two of them.*"

"Shhh," said Alderman Grenfell. And then, as Mrs Hawthorn's words sank in: "Oh, lawks."

"Stop interrupting," snapped Mrs Smee. "We'll have to start again."

A shimmering shape appeared above the table: a majestic young lady with a dramatic bosom, wrapped in a wide and out-of-fashion black gown, no bonnet in sight, skirts rustling with taffeta.

"What the blazes?" demanded Juno, the Younger Duchess of Storm, staring down at them all. "Why am I—"

She shimmered, and disappeared.

Mrs Hawthorn rose to her feet. "Well, *that* was a disaster," she pronounced to the Royal Society of Mediums. "I don't suppose you know exactly where you sent the mistress of the house?"

~

*J*uno spat and swore, using words she had never even heard before. She tumbled through nothingness, though air and light, caught between Storm North and Ghost Island, not quite in one place or the other, and *oh gods, she had the passenger aboard.* What were these magical shenanigans going to do to her baby?

"You have no right to be here," snarled the voice inside her head, the voice of the woman who would have been her mother-in-law, had she been alive to take the title.

"Flaming buggering shite-chimneys," Juno gasped. "Are you haunting *me* now?"

A ghost haunted a place, or an object. Never a person. But she could feel the other Duchess of Storm inside her skin: taking possession. How long had she been in residence?

No. Juno was having none of it. She had lost her house to this ghost. For one horrible moment today, she thought she had lost her husband.

She was damned if she was going to let some entitled old dead lady take her body and her *child* from her.

"Two can haunt this house," she snarled, and stamped her foot, hard.

The walls solidified around her, taking familiar shape. The staircase. Blue carpet, soft blue linen curtains. It was her entrance hall. She was standing in the entrance hall of Storm North. Both feet securely on the floor. And it was all wrong.

"Enough!" roared Juno. She had never thought of herself as a particularly magical person — small spells, little charms here and there, was all she had ever performed. A touch of sympathetic magic, a dash of preservation charm. But right now, she felt magical power boiling up inside her. She did not know where it had come from. But she knew what she wanted to do with it.

She raised her arms, and the carpet bled red. The banisters stained darker, with those pretty gilded fixings she had chosen personally. The curtains shimmered, red velvet instead of blue linen. The old wallpaper, recently refreshed, peeled away to show the bright cream-and-gold pattern she loved underneath.

"This is my bloody house," she declared, and made her way up the staircase.

She found Aunt Seabourne on the landing, wrapped in ivy.

"Where is your sister?" Juno demanded as she untangled Henry's aunt, her hands shaking on the vines.

"Oh, my dear," said Aunt Seabourne, looking smaller than she ever had before. She gave Juno a pitying glance and then darted a glance across at the large mirror that hung on the wall. It had an enormous gilt frame covered in owls and peacock feather designs. Juno had never got rid of it, mostly because Henry looked like a kicked kitten when she suggested it.

She saw herself in the mirror. Pale, too thin around the cheeks to be entirely familiar, wrapped in the most unflattering black dress she had ever worn. Juno Brooks Jupiter. Duchess of Storm.

"Is she really inside me?" she asked plaintively.

"I don't think there's anywhere in this house she is not," said Aunt Seabourne shakily. "I am sorry, my dear. I don't know what to do."

"But you always know what to do."

"Not when it comes to my sisters. They are my weakness, I'm afraid. Seabourne women have always been a force unto themselves." She gave a short, uncomfortable laugh, then reached out a hand, squeezing Juno's. "But of course. You're a Seabourne now, too. I know Henry doesn't have the name. But marriage is a powerful ritual." She gave Juno a watery smile with a little nod of her head in the direction of the belly curve. "And there's the other one. She'll be Seabourne, through and through."

"You think I'm having a girl?" Juno had been so caught up in the thought of 'heir' that it never occurred to her. Oh, gods and hellfire. She was going to give birth to a Seabourne.

Aunt Seabourne gave her an encouraging smile. "You can never tell these things for certain, no matter what the hedgewitches and midwives and all those doctors claim. But Henry was the first boy born to a Seabourne in five generations. Your chances are high for a daughter."

Juno pressed her hand over the curve of her stomach. "Not the next Duke of Storm," she murmured.

"A Duchess, perhaps, in time. A very long time, I hope."

The baby made a wriggling, kicking sort of motion, showing good timing if nothing else.

Juno hadn't allowed herself to think of it as a baby before today. Now she could not stop thinking about it.

"I need to get this ghost out of my house," she said. *And out of myself.* "I don't care if she's Henry's mother, or your sister, or if she doesn't think I'm good enough to be here. I want her out."

"There's the spirit," said Aunt Seabourne. "What do you have in mind?"

~

Despite her long and complex history with ghosts, Juno had never actually exorcised one. She had read about it, in her early days of desperate research.

There were many and various methods. Some involved priests and temples. Some involved water, or salt, or ritual speeches.

Juno had always rather thought that the various exorcism traditions sounded a lot more like sympathetic magic than anything else. Which made sense, because a haunting was like that, too. All symbolism and feelings and *spirit*.

People threw open their windows and shook ghosts out with the bedsheets. They painted sigils on the walls to take control and ownership of those walls, and to force an unwelcome spirit away. They burned the will or smashed the pocket watch that tethered the ghost to the mortal world.

Juno started with the attics, and a broom. "You don't belong here," she told the Duchess in her head in the firmest possible voice. "This is my time. My house. My family. If you were still alive, I would offer you some form of dowager accommodations, but you are not. So, you cannot stay."

She swept with her broom, and spoke aloud: infusing the sweeping motions with her magic, and with her growing confidence.

"I am the Duchess of Storm," she informed the polished stairs. "This is my home. No ghosts allowed."

Once she was about halfway down the house (realising only belatedly quite how many rooms and floors there were, and wishing she had not sent Aunt Seabourne downstairs to wait for her), Juno heard a commotion in the Great Library, and flung the doors open.

"What are you lot doing in there?"

Henry turned wildly towards her. "Juno!" He was with Mneme, Dominic and Thornbury, all looking somewhat tousled and out of breath having just come through the portal. "You're safe."

"The day's not over," she said tartly. "I'm busy duchessing right now, Henry. Perhaps you could wait for me over at Tempest Manse. The servants are gone, so there's no tea, and you'll only get in the way."

His face darkened. "We came here to rescue you. I'm not leaving you alone in this…"

"My house," she said firmly. "This isn't duke business, darling. I'll let you know when I'm done."

"But, Juno!"

She shut the door firmly and continued down the stairs with her broom.

"I am the Duchess of Storm. This is my home. No ghosts allowed."

At every landing she felt a greater sense of peace and confidence wash over her. She could do this.

She did not meet resistance until she set foot on the top of the final staircase. The wallpaper flickered back and forth. The curtains became red, blue, red, blue.

"Enough!" Juno snapped, and swept harder.

Her dress caught on fire.

She gasped, bracing herself against the heat of it. She dropped to the last landing before the ground floor, and rolled against the carpet, trying to smother the flames. A vase tipped over, and Juno threw herself under it so the water put out the fire. "How dare you!" she screamed at the ceiling, when all was smoke and damp black taffeta. "I AM CARRYING YOUR GRANDCHILD!"

Her limbs tightened as the other Duchess took hold of

her body. *Not good enough*, the ghost sneered. *Not duchess enough*.

"That is a matter of opinion," Juno hurled back. Unsteadily, she got to her feet again, and reached for her broom. "Luckily for me, your opinion means nothing here, in this house, *which is mine*."

She swept, and stepped, all the way until she reached the parquet floor of the entrance lobby. She kept sweeping all the way to the double doors.

Aunt Seabourne opened them, as Juno approached. "Are you sure?" she asked.

"I am," Juno replied haughtily. "Extremely good at this, actually."

Confidence meant a lot, when it came to ghosts. Juno was tired of feeling *less than*.

She swept the old Duchess of Storm all the way out of the front door, and outside the house. Something shivered through her: cold and hot at the same time. Whatever connection there was between Juno and her mother-in-law, she felt it break. Juno's hair fanned out wildly, flying free of its pins as the ghost finally left her.

The black taffeta gown dissolved, tearing away in a greyish vapour of threads to reveal Juno's favourite teagown, russet with a creamy trim, and a thick golden pelisse to ward off the autumn chill.

Juno had never seen this particular garment before, but somehow she knew it had a reasonable number of pockets, securely tied in discreet places.

Outside, the autumn leaves on the nearby trees left their branches in a single moment, all at once. *Whump* as they hit the ground.

Antiope Seabourne, former-dead-dowager-old Duchess of Storm, stood on the doorstep, so pale you could see the lines of the tree branches through her, glaring as if about to storm the barricades all over again. "This is not over," she declared.

"Please stop being so unreasonable, Antiope," said Aunt Seabourne to her sister. "The dead must always give way to the living. You said so yourself when you married your Duke of Storm."

"This is different, Galatea!"

"How? The old Duchess gave you just as much trouble as you're giving poor dear Juno. That's why you cursed your wedding ring in the first place."

"Wait," said Juno. "What?"

Aunt Seabourne glanced back into the house and sighed. "Oh dear. Here they come."

Juno turned. She was astonished to see a wave of haughty older ladies sweeping down the staircase behind her. Some had broad skirts and high wigs, like her mother-in-law. Others wore all manner of outlandish, vintage fashions: scooped tapestry corsets and sleeves that draped to the ground. Cleavage windows and high-heeled boots and lace cuffs, neck ruffs; one even wore a man's doublet and hose, her sword gleaming with rubies. Centuries of high fashion, draped with jewels and extravagant hairstyles, thundering in her direction.

"Oh gods," she said faintly. "Duchesses. So many duchesses."

Duchesses of Storm, to be exact. Thirteen of them. Juno recognised many of their faces from the dustier portraits in the library.

The Teacup Isles only had a small handful of duchesses at a time, most of them currently far older than Juno. She did her best to avoid them.

This, right now, was her worst nightmare.

But no, she realised as she saw the uncertain look on Antiope's face. This wasn't *her* nightmare at all.

The leader of the tidal wave of old duchesses was a tall woman, fine-boned, in a high silver wig and matching gown, so tightly corseted that she looked like a porcelain doll. Her wide, layered skirts of ivory lace and petal-pink velvet did a far better job of sweeping the floor than Juno with her makeshift broom.

"Antiope Seabourne," declared this, particularly terrifying Duchess of Storm. "Still making trouble?"

"I got rid of you!" screamed the ghost. "You can't still be here!"

The duchesses sighed and clucked amongst each other, rolling their eyes at her.

"You never did understand," said the leader of the duchesses. This must be Antiope's own mother-in-law. What was her name? Cornelia. Constanzia? Henry only referred to her as his terrifying Grandmamma Jupiter: the reason they had so many libraries. "You Seabournes always think you're better than everyone else. If you marry into the Jupiter line, you have to accept *our* magic. And Jupiter women are extremely attached to their homes."

Juno winced, glancing over at Aunt Seabourne, who wrapped her shawl thoroughly around her, shivering.

Grandmamma Jupiter gave Juno a superior sort of look. "Don't worry, dear. We won't get under your feet. You're the Duchess of Storm, now. We respect that. Antiope will accept it too — eventually."

And then the sea, the storm, the flood of duchesses poured over the threshold, filling the space between Antiope and Juno. As they walked into the rain, they vanished, each of them. Antiope gave one last frustrated look at her sister and daughter-in-law, and vanished along with them.

No transient vapour, Juno noticed, taking a deep breath. No sign that they were passing on, or finding their true release from the mortal coil, or whatever terminology suited.

They were merely taking their leave. For now.

"Aunt Seabourne," she said in a small voice. "Could you please do me a favour, and pop over to the Hare and Wicket? I believe my housekeeper, Mrs Hawthorn, is awaiting me there. Send her across, when she has a moment. And perhaps you might check on Henry at Tempest Manse? He and Mneme are more than welcome to join me in the Lilac Parlour, along with Mr Thornbury Seabourne and Mr Von Trask, when they all have a moment."

Her aunt-in-law gave her perhaps the most sympathetic look she ever had in the entire span of their relationship. She then dropped into a curtsey that was, if not quite meet-the-queen depth, more than respectable. "Certainly, my dear duchess," she said.

Juno bobbed her head in gratitude to her aunt by marriage, went back inside and with some effort, closed the heavy doors behind her.

Alone in her house, she let herself have a bit of a cry, just for a moment. Three sobs maximum, and several deep breaths.

Then she lifted her head up high, and made her way to the Lilac Parlour. The one that was on the ground floor (no more stairs for her today!) with all the very comfy chairs. There was likely to be a lot of conversation to be had, once Henry and the others returned to Storm North.

Juno was dashed if she wasn't going to have her feet up when they arrived.

19

CLEAR SKIES AHEAD

*W*hen in doubt, tea.

Juno sat in her favourite chair: the one covered with lilacs and oak leaf upholstery. Her feet rested on a matching tapestry ottoman. She did not want to move for the rest of her life.

The baby had other ideas: the passenger was turning cartwheels, or performing country dances, or something else that required a great deal of movement.

Aunt Seabourne was helping Mrs Hawthorn set the house to rights, which included shooing away several interfering members of the Royal Society of Mediums, and summoning back all the servants.

Juno thought that she should be the one dealing with such things, but both ladies assured her they had it well in hand: she would not be conceding any duchess territory if she stayed in her comfortable chair with her feet up, and a nice cup of tea.

Henry refused to leave Juno's side. Mneme and Thornbury only stayed a little while before heading out again to deliver the bottle of transient vapour to Gundrow's and get a more accurate estimate on when the family ring could be mended. Juno's ad hoc exorcism had worked for now, but they would all feel much safer when the family ring was doing its job once more.

"I believe there is something about this house in particular that encourages ghostly activity," Henry said apologetically. "A history of strange leylines or particularly fierce spiritual power?"

"They probably didn't bank on your father marrying a Seabourne," said Mneme, on her way out. "According to Mamma, strong-willed magical women make particularly active ghosts."

"Well then," said Henry, meeting the gaze of his wife. "We'd better keep the current Duchess of Storm alive as long as possible, hadn't we?"

Juno snorted. Then she ate two almond shortbreads, because she was a duchess, and pregnant, and no one was going to tell her she should not.

After Mneme and Thornbury left, there remained the very awkward triangle of Juno, Henry, and Dominic.

The assassin — Queen's man — *Ghost* — looked remarkably comfortable on the very frilly couch that belonged to this parlour. He probably blended in everywhere.

"Tell me," said Juno. "Did you manage to do anything about those assassins hired to kill my husband?"

"You really don't have to worry about—" Henry began, but Juno held up her hand.

"Darling. The time of protecting me is over. If I am to remain calm, and safe, and unbothered between now and the birth of our child, I can't be worried about whatever secret dangers are going on behind my back." Juno crossed her arms, and ate another biscuit. "Dominic?"

The man in black glanced between the two of them. "I

made a full report to head office," he said. "Now we know the money came from Trevental, it's a little easier to track who took the job. The agents responsible for the attack on the *Majestic Harvest* have been rounded up."

"And that's what you are," Juno said evenly. "An agent. Or are you still an assassin?"

"Juno, this is Crown business," Henry said in a pained voice.

She lifted a hand. "You are retired, on the verge of becoming a father. But somehow you keep being dragged out to missions and playing in politics and nearly getting assassinated. As far as I'm concerned, this is *family* business." She gave Dominic a sharp look. "Tell me he's safe and I'll believe you."

"He'll be safe if he stays home," said Dominic quickly.

Henry made a protesting noise "Now, look here."

Dominic and Juno gave him equally scathing looks.

"There are protections laid on family manors like these," said Dominic. "Generations of protection. Give us a couple of weeks to be sure we've tracked down all of the Trevental assassins, and sorted out this business with Boris Lerange. It's going to be a diplomatic nightmare," he added with a wince.

"Which is exactly why I should—" Henry began.

"*No,*" Dominic and Juno said in unison.

Henry rose, grumbling, and poured himself some more tea.

Dominic held out his cup, eyebrows raised.

Grumbling even more, Henry filled it for him.

"How long have you two worked together?" Juno asked. They clearly were more familiar with each other than she had realised.

"I didn't know he was a Von Trask," Henry said immediately. "You could have mentioned the relationship when I got married," he added to Dominic, sounding put out.

"Information is power," Dominic replied with an arch of his eyebrows. "Our paths have crossed now and then," he added to Juno. "But we don't get put on the same jobs very often. Some of us get the missions that involve royal balls and ratafia and smiling at everyone, and others get the real work behind the scenes."

"And that's where the Ghost comes in?"

Dominic's face darkened a little. "The Ghost was my father," he said, and it was as if all the warmth bled out of the room. "A family tradition of sorts."

"But you don't kill people?"

His face did not shift. "Sometimes I do. If the wish of the customer is in the Crown's best interest. Sometimes, someone else covers the job for me so that it looks as if the assassination took place. And sometimes… well, sometimes, it is very useful indeed to know that someone wants a very important person out of the way." He glanced at Henry, who made a 'pish-posh' sort of gesture, making light of the possibility that he counted as important.

"Your father, though," Juno said slowly. "Bertram wasn't an agent of the Crown."

Dominic laughed in genuine surprise. "Gods, no. He was just a very, very bad man."

She thought about the cellar, and shivered. Bertram Van Trask wasn't the only one who did bad things. None of their hands were clean — not Dominic, Vance or Will. Did it matter, that her husband's brothers had tried so hard to escape their father's sinister business? Did it matter that Vance had not?

"I didn't know about it until after his death," Dominic went on. "I found the portal ring among his effects, and a journal chronicling his — shall we say, work?" This time his laugh sounded less humorous, more bitter. "I had thought there were no more nasty surprises left in our family. I had a plan for what I would do with my life, now I was free of him. I'd already qualified as a magister. I had an offer to continue with postgraduate work, specialise in necromancy. But I had another offer on the table, too." His eyes flicked towards Henry.

"Ah," said Henry, understanding. "The Queen's Consultant. Convincing sort of bastard, isn't he?"

Juno was not supposed to know that Henry's former employer, the Queen's Consultant, was also the spymaster. Apparently, they were sharing all their secrets today. Keeping it in the family, at least.

"I took the Ghost's journal to the palace," said Dominic. "There was one entry in particular that shed light on an incident during the summer of the Queen's coronation year. I thought they'd find it useful, not that they'd offer me a *job*."

Juno bit her lip. Vance's hunting accident had happened that summer. "Tell me," she said.

"According to the journal, the Ghost was training an apprentice to take his place. The two of them had successfully enacted two kills together, on foreign soil. He didn't like to bring his business too close to home. But the Troilish Empire hired the Ghost to take out a hit on a very high profile local target."

"The Queen's summer tour," said Henry. It was a voice Juno had never quite heard him use before — short, sharp, professional. None of his usual flair, or humour. "She was sailing by swan-shaped boat to visit each of the islands in turn. At the Isle of Glass, there was a sudden squall — an unnatural storm, the magisters said afterwards. I was supposed to be on that tour with the Queen, new Duke of Storm and all that, but my mother needed me at home. They sent Thornbury instead. Good thing too, as it happened. Needed an extra spellcracker on that ship, not a diplomat. The ship would have gone down, if they hadn't managed to turn the magical storm against whoever sent it…" He trailed off, looking awkward.

"Needless to say," Dominic said dryly. "The assassination attempt failed. Badly. I honestly don't know if Vance tried to stop it, or if his death was some kind of stupid accident."

"Why would your father choose *Vance* as his apprentice?" Juno blurted out. "As an assassin? I can't picture it."

Vance had remembered, though. He had finally remembered his death because they were on a ship under magical attack.

Dominic shrugged. "Vance was the only one of the three of us who never said no to him. Father despised him for it, but after Will jumped ship, he started reconsidering how useful it was: that Vance was so scared of him. I knew something shady had happened, when Father returned to the hunting lodge with Vance's body. But something shady was always happening."

Juno sat very still, considering the possibility that if Vance had not died that night, her life would have been very, very different. She might still be married to a murderer, for a start.

"I think," she said after a moment. "I owe Thornbury some kind of fruit basket. Don't you think, dear?"

Henry patted her on the arm. "They're in need of furniture, over at Tempest Manse, rather than fruit. Let's send them lots of chairs."

The baby kicked again. Juno placed her hand over her stomach, allowing herself to be glad for this life, right here. The one she had stumbled across, quite impulsively, on a day full of chaos and cake fights. "I'm sorry for your loss," she said to Dominic.

He was getting better at smiling around her. This time, it reached his eyes. "You don't have to be," he told her. "I think it all worked out for the best."

~

*J*uno was almost relaxed. She drank more tea, and listened idly as her husband and brother-in-law discussed the diplomatic implications of the Trevental revelation.

Outside the windows of the Lilac Parlour, the rain, which had eased a little, became heavier. It did not matter. She was going nowhere.

Somewhere on this level of the house, she could hear a deep thumping sound. Then at the same time, some sort of commotion upstairs.

Dominic pricked up his ears. "You definitely swept all the ghosts out?" he asked Juno.

"Well, I thought so," she replied huffily.

"That's someone at the front door," said Henry, hopping to his feet. "No butlers yet, m'dear?"

"I believe they took themselves all off together on some sort of golf-related holiday," said Juno. "But Mrs Hawthorn is around."

"Mrs Hawthorn has never answered a door in her life," said the Duke of Storm, already bounding out of the parlour. "Some things are beyond the pale, Juno!"

Juno sighed, and stared at her tapestry ottoman, currently holding her feet. It was so very, very comfortable.

"You could stay here," said Dominic, already holding out a hand to help her up. "And not find out what is going on as quickly as everyone else."

Slowly and grumpily, Juno accepted his assistance. "They promised me the life of a duchess was all sweetmeats and luxury," she muttered.

"You'd have hated that," he shot back.

"Show's what you know! I am exceptional at sweetmeats and luxury."

~

As Juno and Dominic reached the hall, Mneme and Thornbury clattered down the stairs from above, looking drenched and frantic. They had a scrawny, rumpled figure with them who Juno recognised after a bemused moment as Mr Marlborough.

Apparently Henry had abandoned his valet somewhere. She would not feel smug about that, not at all.

"Henry!" said Mneme. "We've had word from the camp at Ghost Island. The Queen has gone missing."

Henry, busily trying to manage all the bolts and such on the heavy front door, still being assailed by thumping from the other side, rocked back on his heels. "What? Kidnapped?"

"Might be worse than that," said Thornbury.

"What's worse than kidnapped?"

Mneme and Thornbury winced, sharing one of those *very married* looks that they had somehow already cultivated, despite being husband and wife for only a few months.

"Eloped," said Mneme finally, when it became clear her husband had no intention of saying it aloud. "Everyone's saying that her majesty eloped."

"Mneme!" declared Aunt Seabourne, emerging from the kitchen door where she had been conferring with Mrs Hawthorn. "What on earth are you saying, young lady? Queens don't elope."

The banging on the front door continued unabated.

"It sounds too bloody good to be true," Henry said under his breath.

"Henry!" said Aunt Seabourne in a shocked gasp.

"Well, I'm sorry, aunt, but I mean it." Henry threw up his hands in impatience. "We've been chasing our tails after her blessed majesty and this misguided plot to nab a foreign suitor for months, which is *bound* to lead to disaster, and if it turns out she and Manticore have finally got their act together, I couldn't be happier for them."

"STORM!" bellowed a voice from the other side of the front door. "*STORM!*"

Henry, still caught in the fervour of his own righteous speech, looked utterly crestfallen. "Balls," he muttered.

Juno could not agree more with the sentiment. Since no one else was making a move, she walked very carefully across her entrance hall, stepped around her husband, and pulled the heavy door open herself.

Lord Manticore, soaked to the skin from the rain, lurched inside like a man possessed.

"She's gone," he gasped. "The crew of the *Caliban* took them. She could be married by now. It's all over."

Dominic winced. Juno met his gaze briefly, thinking of his brother.

"Oh my," said Aunt Seabourne, looking around for a bench to collapse on. "*Our Queen?*"

Henry opened and shut his mouth. "Manticore," he said faintly, voicing what they were all thinking. "If the Queen didn't elope with you… who exactly is she planning to marry?"

The silence that followed his question was deafening.

～

The most important thing about being a duchess, Juno had come to realise, was knowing exactly when to put your foot down.

In this instance, putting her foot down meant standing between her wild-eyed husband and the library portal.

"No," she said.

"Get out of our way, Duchess," snarled Lord Manticore.

Juno smiled politely at him. "I have no objection to your quest, my lord. I wish you well of it. But you are not taking my husband with you."

"Darling, I have to go," said Henry, looking pained. "I serve the Queen."

"The Queen has made her intentions very clear," Juno replied. "As have the assassins that are still set against you. I will not allow you to leave this house until I know you will be safe." She placed her hands on her stomach, and glared at them both.

"Juno," said Henry helplessly. "Be reasonable."

"Move her aside," Lord Manticore insisted, only to be met with disdainful looks from every woman in the room. "This is a diplomatic emergency."

"Is it an emergency?" Mneme spoke up. "The Queen left on one of her own privateer ships. She is surrounded by her own people. If she wants to select a husband without all the usual pomp and ceremony, I'm not sure any of us can stop her."

"That's why I need him," Lord Manticore said, gesticulating in Henry's general direction. "Everyone knows that the Duke of Storm is the only one the Queen really listens to."

"Well!" said Juno acidly. "Perhaps the rest of you had

better work on your communication skills. The Duke of Storm is not currently available."

Dominic had rather slowly been edging towards the portal until he stood at Juno's side. She gave him a sidelong look, guessing he was the only gentleman in the room ruthless enough to move her. He addressed Henry, however, not Juno: she realised to her complete shock that he was on her side in more ways than one.

"Your grace," said Dominic, sounding remarkably stern. "We all serve the Crown. I personally am willing to go along with whatever Lord Manticore suggests. But if you choose to go haring off into deliberate danger, leaving the protections of this house and abandoning my sister in her condition…"

Juno placed a hand on his arm before he could get to the threat part of his sentence. "That's very touching, Dominic, but I can handle this." She smiled at her husband with a ferocity that clearly took him aback. "Dearest, if you go haring off into deliberate danger, leaving the protections of this house, and get yourself killed by assassins, I will personally burn all three of your houses to the ground."

There was a strangled pause in the room..

"Good gods," muttered Lord Manticore in a very quiet voice.

Henry beamed as if Juno had declared her undying love for him. With a flourish, he turned away from the portal. "Sorry, Manticore. You heard the lady. I'm needed at home. Retired from active service, you know. Give my best regards to her majesty, when you find her." He swooped around, and kissed Juno in front of everyone.

It was a very thorough embrace.

"Henry," Thornbury said politely, after a few moments. "Do you think perhaps you two could take this a few steps away from the portal? The rest of us have some Queen-related diplomacy to undertake."

"Oh, yes," said Henry cheerfully, wrapping an arm as far around Juno as he could currently manage, and sweeping her to one side. "Carry on, all of you."

Gradually, the library emptied of their guests. Most of them, including Dominic, went through the portal with Lord Manticore. Aunt Seabourne withdrew back in the direction of the kitchens.

Juno, warm in the embrace of her husband, hardly noticed them all leave.

"Henry," she murmured some time later, after they had removed themselves to a chair in the corner of the library. "I think some redecoration is in order. The second floor needs a complete redesign. Colour palette. Wallpaper. Furniture. Everything."

"Whatever you say, Duchess," he replied, hands busy beneath the layers of her clothing. "Gods above. How many pockets do you have in this garment?"

METIS SEABOURNE, CAPTAIN BONES, QUEEN AUD, LORD
MANTICORE, MRS & MRS SEABOURNE
AND THE CREW OF THE *CALIBAN* WILL RETURN
IN THE 6TH TEACUP MAGIC NOVELLA:
THIS ENCHANTED ISLAND
COMING SOON

BUT FOR NOW, KEEP READING FOR A LITTLE MORE JUNO

20

SQUALLING

alliope Opal Jupiter, heir to the duchy of Storm, was born at the end of January, during a particularly fierce winter. The week before her birth included a blizzard, a freak hailstorm, several frozen pipes, and a rise in the popularity of warming charms at Storm North, as well as the surrounding village.

The baby had a very red face, to match her bright red hair. She cried almost constantly for the first two days. After that, she settled into an amiable but spirited personality that left her shell-shocked parents a touch discombobulated.

Visitors were discouraged for the first few weeks, then heartily encouraged after that.

Mneme and Thornbury declared themselves aunt and uncle.

Agate and Amethyst promptly declared themselves aunts too, if cousins were going to be allowed such liberties. During their first visit, when the two of them gathered around the crib to coo at the newcomer, Juno slipped her wedding ring off, stashing it in one of the many pockets she had tied on to her favourite tea gown.

Free from the Jupiter family protections for a moment, Juno saw her dead cousin Opal bestow a kiss on the forehead of her namesake, which made her smile. Then, very quickly, she slid the ring back on to her finger. Once couldn't be too careful, after all.

She did not regret asking the jewellers of Gundrow's to make the 'ghost-banishing curse' a little less intense than the version that Antiope had placed upon the wedding ring during her own time as Duchess of Storm. Ghosts had their place in the world. As long as Juno could choose whether or not to visit that place, she was content.

Four weeks after the arrival of little Calliope, Dominic came to tea at Juno's invitation. She suggested that he might also consider himself an uncle, if he liked.

(This had been a matter of some agonising on her part, but she resolved in the end that if one had to have an assassin in the family, it was best to ensure he had as many reasons as possible to protect one's children.)

Dominic frowned thoughtfully, and said nothing for or against the idea. But when Calliope turned one, and on every naming day thereafter, a mysterious parcel would arrive, bearing a spiral skull seal upon it, always containing a most extravagant and impractical gift for the eldest Jupiter child.

Captain J. Willoughby Bones did not take up the same offer, sent by folded (waterproof) paper bird across the ocean: to be an official uncle to Calliope. A baby gift arrived from Bosun Blythe, however: a large, pearl-pink seashell that whispered sea shanties if you listened hard enough to it.

Juno put it on a shelf for now, because Calliope kept

trying to gnaw on the thing, but she appreciated the gesture.

~

When Calliope was seven years old, Juno left her on a picnic rug in the garden for a mere moment while she chased two of her younger daughters, Melpomene and Polyhymnia, out of a rosebush. When she returned with a toddler under each arm, she discovered her eldest sitting in place, talking quietly into thin air.

"Cally," Juno said gently, sitting down in a heap with the little ones on her lap. "Who are you talking to?"

"Grandmamma," Calliope informed her.

Juno took a deep breath, and counted to six. She checked the ruby ring on her finger, which looked flawless and perfect but somehow was *no longer sufficient for purpose.* "And does your grandmamma have anything to say to me?" she asked finally.

"The maids keep forgetting to dust the bureau in the Sage Room," said Calliope. "Also, she misses the peacocks. Can we get peacocks?"

"I'll think about it," said Juno, with a sigh. "Perhaps you can tell your grandmamma she needn't worry about the bureau, or anything else in this house. I have it all well in hand."

Calliope nodded, playing with her hair. "She heard you," she added. "She says she's not ready to go yet. But you're doing fine."

"Oh," said Juno. That shouldn't make her feel like crying, but it very much did. "That's good to know, darling. Shall we go in? Mina and Polly need their naps."

"Not yet," said Calliope, leaning against her arm.

"Grandmamma has some very funny stories about when Dada was young. Can I stay longer?"

Juno kissed Calliope on the top of her head. "Just a little longer. But you don't have to hear all the stories today." She sighed, and gazed across the grass. "Grandmamma isn't going anywhere."

THE END

Tea & Sympathetic Magic

There's nothing more dangerous than an eligible duke...

Every eligible young lady of the Teacup Isles wants to marry the Duke of Storm, except Miss Mnemosyne Seabourne, who is quite content on the shelf, thank you very much. All she wants is a quiet life and a good book.

At a house party full of ruthless debutantes willing to employ sneaky sympathetic magic to win a husband of quality, Mneme joins forces with an enigmatic spellcracker to rescue the duke from being married against his will.

Can Mneme save the Duke of Storm without becoming his bride? Will this caper ruin her reputation forever? Can teacups and hedgehogs be used as projectile weapons in emergencies? Why are attractive men more devastating when they roll up their sleeves?

If you enjoy Regency house parties, witty romantic banter and high society sorcery, you'll adore this magical comedy of manners cosy mystery novella.

The Frost Fair Affair

Our heroine stumbles across a precarious plot while printing political pamphlets...

Thanks to last Season's scandal involving her family, Miss Mnemosyne Seabourne is officially notorious. Wintering in Town, she hopes to use her new celebrity to campaign about the unfair restriction on portal travel for ladies… while being quietly courted by a certain handsome spellcracker.

As the river freezes over and a spectacular Frost Fair sets up on the ice, Mneme finds herself beset by secret societies, spies and sneaky saboteurs. Who stole her political pamphlets? Who is leaving dead bodies around printing presses for anyone to find?

Mr Thornbury knows more than he's letting on. If she can't trust the man she hoped to marry, Mneme is just going to have to unravel the mystery for herself, quick enough to save both of their lives.

If you enjoy vintage spy adventures, flirtatious couples and cosy sleigh rides, you'll adore this exciting sequel novella to *Tea and Sympathetic Magic*.

Spellcracker's Honeymoon

Our honeymooning heroine must unmask a magical murderer.

Happily married, Mrs Mnemosyne Seabourne travels to an island of no magic, for a relaxing honeymoon with her new husband Thornbury.

But the magic-free Isle of Aster is not what it seems. There's a monster roaming the hills, a royal scandal brewing on the horizon, and (of course!) an impossible, magical murder to be solved.

On the night of the Midsummer Masque at the Queen's country palace, Thornbury goes missing, leaving Mneme to unravel a web of secrets and lies involving her own husband.

Who could commit magical murder on an island with no magic? Only a spellcracker...

If you enjoy cozy magical mysteries, glamorous masquerade balls and the art of saucy letter writing, you'll love the third Teacup Magic novella.

Lady Liesl's Seaside Surprise

Spied beside the seaside: stepdaughter seeks scandal!

Lady Liesl, fourth daughter of the Earl of Sandwich, always thought her fate was to marry well, and live a perfect life like her older sisters.

Now she's had a taste of rebellion, and she likes it...

Hunting a missing diamond in a remote seaside town on behalf of a runaway Countess, Liesl finds herself at the mysterious Aphrodite Villa, with a sinister lack of servants, and no household magic in sight... not to mention a parlour full of wild, bohemian artists, including the devilishly seductive Perdita.

This is the Teacup Isles, where nothing is quite as it seems. Lady Liesl is about to uncover some surprising secrets about her family and herself.

If you enjoy cozy magical mysteries, witty banter and Sapphic flirtation by the sea, you'll love this stand-alone novella about one of Mneme Seabourne's dearest friends.

SPARKS & PHILTRES

Light the gaslamps and stand well back! A brand new series of faerie Victoriana fantasy adventures by Tansy Rayner Roberts.

GATE SINISTER (Sparks & Philtres #1)

A governess sets out on a terrible quest, to a country manor that hates her. Two magical engineers flee the city to avoid the Queen's wrath, at the behest of a wicked enchantress.

Britannia is ruled by love philtres and antidotes… but no fairies, as they were sent into exile long ago. And good riddance!

On All Hallows Eve, the Gate Sinister can be opened, and the ways between worlds will be free once more. One night only, to change the world forever.

∾

HOUSE PERILOUS (Sparks & Philtres #2)

Number 12, Acteon Place is more than just a London townhouse. It is a harbour for the most dangerous enchantress in Britannia. There are prisoners in the cellar. Mysterious magical experiments in the attic. A fairy killer on the loose. A hunted governess, desperate to protect the two children she betrayed.

Other features of the house include an excellent cook. Exquisite wallpaper. Slightly homicidal carpet... depending who steps on it. And a yellow cat who provides more questions than answers.

Flavia Wednesday and her friends might not all escape this house alive. For those that do... there are even more perils beyond its walls.